THE WORLD IS FULL OF MARRIED MEN

THE PUBLISHING SENSATION WHICH
TOPPED EVERY BESTSELLER LIST

David Cooper had had other affairs outside his
marriage before but this one was different. Claudia
was emotionally and physically unlike anything he'd
ever met. This time, for the first time, he wished
he was free.

Here is a devastating exposure of the world
of starlets, boozy models, sadistic film producers
and the hangers-on. A novel of the London scene
which the SUNDAY MIRROR called 'not so much
a jungle as a giant sleeping-bag'. A world of phony
showbiz promises, of starlets with no talent and less
principle, of beds being used to sign contracts,
of ageing stars who use girls as a substitute
for hormones.

Revolted or intrigued, this is one book you
can't ignore!

Also by Jackie Collins in *Star*

THE WORLD IS FULL OF MARRIED MEN

Jackie Collins

A STAR BOOK

Published by
the Paperback Division of
W. H. ALLEN & Co. Ltd

A Star Book
Published in 1976
by the Paperback Division of W. H. Allen & Co. Ltd.
A Howard & Wyndham Company
44 Hill Street. London W1X 8LB

This edition reprinted 1979

First published in Great Britain by
W. H. Allen & Co. Ltd.

Copyright © by Jackie Collins 1968

Printed in Great Britain by
C. Nicholls & Company Ltd, The Philips Park Press, Manchester

ISBN 0 352 39875 2

This book is sold subject to the condition that it shall not,
by way of trade or otherwise, be lent, re-sold,
hired out or otherwise circulated without the publisher's prior
consent in any form of binding or cover other than that in which it is
published and without a similar condition including this
condition being imposed on the subsequent purchaser.

CHAPTER ONE

'When I was fifteen, I was a doll, an absolute doll! Mother was terrified to let me out on my own, she felt I was bound to come home pregnant, or something silly like that.'

The speaker was Claudia Parker. The listener was David Cooper. Claudia was in bed. She was a very beautiful girl, and she knew it, and David knew it, so everyone was happy. She had long shiny ash-blonde hair, which fell thickly around her face, and a deep fringe down to her eyebrows, which accentuated her enormous slanty green eyes. The face was perfect, with a small straight nose and luscious full lips. She wore no make-up and no clothes, and she was covered by a thin silk sheet.

David sat at the end of the bed. He was forty, and looked it. He had black slightly curly hair, and a well-lined rugged face. His nose was rather prominent, and he wore thick square horn-rimmed glasses. He was a masculine-looking man, and enjoyed a great deal of success with the opposite sex.

'Well, eventually I left home,' continued Claudia. 'I mean it was all just too impossible and dreary. So, one night I sneaked out, never to return! Actually, I met this marvellous boy, an actor, and he brought me to London with him.' She sighed and wriggled around under the sheet. 'Got a cigarette, darling?'

David produced a packet of filter-tips from his dressing-gown pocket, and handed one to Claudia. She took a long drag. 'Want to hear more of my lurid background?'

'I want to hear everything about you.'

Claudia smiled. 'You're so sweet. Not at all dull. I thought when I first saw you, you would turn out to be an absolute bore. But how wrong I was. I'm mad about you!' She leaned over to where David was sitting, the sheet was left behind, and she wound her arms around his neck, and

5

started to nibble at his ear. She had a fabulous body. David pushed her back on the bed.

'Want me, baby?' she whispered. 'Want me badly?'

David grunted his assent.

Suddenly, she twisted herself free, jumped off the bed, and ran to the door. 'You're too much,' she said, 'but not now, darling. Maybe you can so soon again, but I need a little rest.' She giggled. 'I'm going to have a shower, then maybe we can get some lunch out; and then, baby, then we can come back and make it all night long!'

She vanished through the door, and David heard the water running in the bathroom.

He thought about Claudia, he thought about how they had first met. Was it really only three weeks ago? He had had a particularly hard day at the office, and Linda had been nagging him about all the extra work he seemed to be doing, and how she never saw him any more. It was nearly six, and he was just getting ready to leave, when Phillip Abbottson had come darting into his office. 'Listen, Dave,' he had asked, 'got a spare moment to come down to the studio and make a decision for us? We've got two girls testing for the Beauty Maid soap product, and it's a dead heat; we just can't decide.'

Reluctantly David had gone with Phillip to the ground floor studio in the enormous Cooper-Taylor advertising building. It was owned by his uncle, R. P. Cooper who had two sons, and Sanford Taylor with no sons but a son-in-law. Therefore, David came sixth in the line of importance, which in a business of such a size was quite important, but not important enough as far as David was concerned. He was in charge of the T.V. section and, since Beauty Maid soap was to be featured quite heavily on T.V., it was necessary to pick the right girl. However, Phillip Abbottson usually made the decisions about who was to be featured in the commercials, and David had never found fault yet.

They entered the studio, and David immediately spotted her. She was sprawled in a canvas chair, wearing a white terry cloth robe. Her hair was piled high on her head, and she was eating an apple. The other girl came into focus next. She was chocolate-box pretty, prim and virginal looking. However, her figure belied her face. She had a protruding bust, the largeness of which was emphasized by the flesh-coloured swimsuit she was wearing.

'What tits!' muttered Phillip.

'Well, let them do their stuff,' said David.

Phillip called for silence in the small studio, gestured to the Chocolate Box girl, and she made her way on to the small set where the fake bathroom was located. She climbed daintily into the large round marble bath, flesh colour swimsuit and all, and a prop man rushed eagerly over, and started to spray her ample proportions with bubbles. Someone else thrust a large bar of soap into her hand, and then Phillip shouted, 'O.K., let's take it.'

The cameras started to turn, and David watched the scene on a small closed circuit T.V. screen.

The girl flashed a toothy smile at the camera. 'I'm a Beauty Maid,' she cooed. She lathered the soap in her hands and spread it luxuriously up her arm, first one arm, and then the other. 'Beauty Maid was made for me. It's so creamy, so smooth, so sexy.' She drew one long leg out of the bubbles and lathered that too. 'Why don't you try Beauty Maid, and then you can be a Beauty Maid too!' She smiled at the camera again, and shifted slightly, so that her ample bosom was well in focus.

'O.K., cut it,' shouted Phillip. 'Miss Parker now please.'

David turned to watch as Claudia changed places with the other girl. She had a panther-like grace all her own. Her voice was low and sexy as she read her lines. When she had finished she casually shrugged her way back into her terry cloth robe, and went and sat down. Chocolate Box was still bouncing around the set.

'The Parker girl,' David said to Phillip. 'She's the one.'

As he left the set, Claudia caught his eye. She smiled, and he felt a hint of promise in her smile. He returned to his office, packed up a few papers, called Linda to say he would be home for dinner, and then left.

Claudia was standing outside the building.

'Hello,' she said, 'small world.'

They talked for a few minutes about the tests, and Beauty Maid soap, and the weather, and then David suggested dinner. Claudia said she thought that would be a divine idea.

They went to a small Italian restaurant in Chelsea, where David knew he was unlikely to be spotted by any of his or

7

Linda's friends. He called Linda on the 'phone and made his excuses. She sounded upset but understanding. Claudia called a boy-friend and cancelled him out. They ate cannelloni and talked and held hands, and there it all began.

Suddenly Claudia returned from the bathroom. 'Darling, what have you been doing?' she questioned. David pulled her down on the bed. 'Thinking about you, and how you picked me up.'

'It's not true!' she protested, 'you're just a dirty old man who fancied me as soon as you saw me in that bath!' She was wearing her white terry cloth robe again. David ran his hands underneath it. She shivered. The 'phone rang. 'Saved by the bell!' she giggled, and rolled over to answer it. It was her agent.

David dressed slowly, watching Claudia all the time. She spoke animatedly to her agent, occasionally pausing to stick out a small pink tongue at him. Finally she hung up. 'Oh baby, you're dressed,' she said accusingly. 'I've got simply marvellous news though. I have an interview with Conrad Lee tomorrow. He's over here looking for a completely new face to star in his latest film; it's all about the Virgin Mary or something. Anyway, I'm to see him tomorrow, six p.m., in his suite at the Plaza Carlton. Isn't it all too exciting?'

David wasn't too pleased. 'Why do you have to see him at night, what's wrong with during the day?'

'Oh baby, don't be silly. My God, if he wants to get laid he can get it just as well at eight a.m. as any other time.' She marched crossly over to the dressing-table and meticulously started to apply her make-up.

'All right, I'm sorry I spoke. I just don't know why you want this silly career of yours. Why don't you . . .'

'Why don't I what?' interrupted Claudia coldly. 'Give it all up and marry you? And what do you suggest we do with your wife and kids, and all your other various family entanglements?'

David was silent.

'Look baby.' Her voice softened. 'I don't bug you about things, so just forget it. You don't own me, and I don't own you, and that's the way it should be.' She applied her false eyelashes with a flourish. 'I'm starving, what about lunch?'

They went to their little Italian restaurant, and good

8

humour was restored. 'Sunday's such a dreary day,' said Claudia, 'it sort of sags along.' She drank her red wine with relish, and smiled at the short fat proprietor who grinned happily back. 'Do you know everyone believes they are beautiful, I'm sure of it. They look in the mirror and they see two eyes, a nose and a mouth, and that's it, they think what a gas!' Her laughter lit up the restaurant, and David laughed with her. She was such a beautiful, vital girl. He had had affairs outside marriage before, many times, but this was different; this time, for the first time, he wished he was free.

'I met this man once,' said Claudia. 'He promised me a yacht in the South of France, a villa in Cuba! Lots of jewels and all that jazz, and then he just disappeared. I heard later he was a spy, and got shot. Isn't life funny....'

After lunch they drove through the West End looking for a film they would like to see.

'Look at all those nuts,' exclaimed Claudia, watching a large procession heading towards Trafalgar Square. 'Can you imagine spending all your spare time rushing around tying yourself to Embassies, and sitting down all over the place? And all the fella's have beards. I wonder why ...?' She snuggled up closer to David. 'Let's forget the movie, let's go back to my place and swing.'

CHAPTER TWO

'Ban the Bomb,' the banner attached to the stout lady's back announced quite clearly.

'Peace everywhere,' declared a large notice held aloft by a bearded young man.

'End Nuclear Warfare,' stated a large piece of cardboard clutched gamely by a harassed woman, also clutching two scruffy children by the hand.

This group, along with several hundred others, marched

9

slowly into Trafalgar Square. Many had arrived before them, and there was a milling crowd round about Nelson's Column and the fountains. Linda Cooper was already there; she stood squashed between an earnest-looking group of young girls with long, untidy hair, and grubby-looking outfits, and a bespectacled gentleman, who kept up a constant muttering to himself.

An attractive woman in her early thirties, with short auburn hair partly concealed beneath a chiffon scarf, she wore a cream Chanel suit which looked out of place in the company she was with. One would imagine that ten years earlier she had been very pretty indeed, but the prettiness had been replaced with an expression of the acceptance of life. There were little lines, a certain amount of tiredness and slightly too much make-up; but the overall effect somehow seemed to make her more attractive.

She glanced around her; it seemed so funny to be standing there, part of the crowd, without David. It was so seldom that she did anything or went anywhere without him, but more and more lately there had been long business trips, and late meetings, and he seemed to have become so completely involved in his work, almost to the exclusion of all else. She sighed. It was only by chance really that she was at the meeting today. David was away, and suddenly she felt she must get out of the house and do something different for a change. The children were in the country with her parents for the week-end; she had declined to go, thinking that David would be home, but at the last moment he had had to rush off as usual. She had found herself all alone, and eventually decided she couldn't bear to sit around the house all day, so she had 'phoned Monica and Jack and they had asked her over to lunch. But it was a mistake; they were really David's friends from his bachelor days and she always sensed a certain forced gaiety about them, a sort of 'so David finally married you' attitude, 'well, he could have done worse'. After an hour and a half she excused herself on the pretext that she had to get home, there was so much to be done before the children arrived. What, she could not imagine, but Monica and Jack didn't argue, so she left.

It was while she was driving home that she noticed the marchers and the banners and the crowds, and it was on impulse she parked her Mini in a side street and made her

10

way into Trafalgar Square, which appeared to be the general gathering point.

It was a subject she had often thought about, and secretly wished that she could be part of. To protest seemed the very least one could do, if not for oneself for one's children.

The bespectacled man standing beside her suddenly looked at his watch. 'It's three o'clock,' he announced excitedly.

There was a sudden surge forward of the crowd, and a general shouting and yelling, and small groups of people seemed to disintegrate from the mass and rush towards the road where they promptly sat down in front of the traffic. Linda was carried forward with the crush and found herself near the edge of the pavement. There were a lot of policemen pushing and dragging and lifting the squatters from the road and as soon as one person was removed another immediately took his place. The mob was delighted. They chanted various slogans and cheered and booed the police. The large blue police vans gradually began to fill up, but still undaunted new squatters appeared.

Linda felt marvellous. 'Ban the Bomb,' she shouted. *She* was protesting about the bomb. *She* was actually involved in a meeting of world wide interest. *She* was in a minute way helping to protect the future of her children. It was an exciting experience.

'Ban the Bomb,' joined in the people near her.

'Come on, darlin',' a dark-haired young man grabbed her by the arm, and together they rushed on to the road. They sat in the face of an oncoming taxi and the irate taxi-driver growled, 'Bloody barmy, the lot of 'em.' Linda had a feeling of complete exhilaration, and then a pink faced constable was grabbing her under the arms and pulling her to the side of the road. She started to struggle and another policeman joined them and took hold of her legs. There was a moment of immodesty as she felt her skirt hike up above her waist, and then they unceremoniously dumped her back on the pavement.

Helping hands got her to her feet where she discovered she had lost her shoes and somehow or other cut her arm. Her scarf had vanished and her hair fell around her face.

'Well, you look a right mess,' it was the dark-haired young man again, 'want to give it another bash?'

A girl grabbed him by the arm. 'Oh, come on, Paul,' she said, 'let's go. We don't want to get lumbered down to Bow

11

Street again.' She was very small, with long lank pale yellow hair, and she was very young.

Paul ignored her. 'Look,' he said to Linda, 'you had better come with us. I've got a mate lives near here and we can maybe get you some shoes.'

'Well . . .' started Linda.

'Oh, come on, Paul,' said the girl crossly.

'Well all right,' decided Linda, and the three of them started to push their way to the edge of the crowd. Paul took hold of Linda's arm and guided her through the mass of people, his lank-haired girl-friend trailed miserably behind.

'My name's Paul Bedford, what's yours?'

Linda glanced at him. He was tall, with slate grey eyes. She guessed he must be about twenty-two. She found him uncomfortably attractive.

'Mrs. Cooper,' she said firmly.

He gave her an odd look, half-amused, half puzzled. 'All right, Mrs. Cooper.'

The pavement was cold and hard on Linda's stockinged feet, and suddenly she found herself wishing she was safely home, and not rushing around Trafalgar Square with some strange young man whom she had only met ten minutes before.

'Listen, I have a car parked close by,' she said, 'I think it would be better if I got back to it. I'm sure I have some old shoes in it.'

But Paul was already leading her across the road into Newport Street. 'We're here,' he said, banging on a battered yellow door, 'at least come up and we'll bandage your arm and then I'll take you back to your car.'

The girl-friend looked sulky in the background.

'All right,' said Linda.

A make-up-less, white-faced, blackhaired girl finally came to the front door. She wore a slightly tattered-looking blue and gold brocade Chinese housecoat and once-white fur slippers. 'Hi baby,' she greeted Paul brightly, 'and how's little Mel,' she nodded at the girl-friend. 'Come on up.'

They followed her up a narrow staircase into an enormous room painted completely black. There was a large bed in one corner, a lot of books and cushions scattered and piled around and a record player with Miles Davis turned

12

up full volume. This appeared to be the entire extent of the furnishings of the room.

'Where's the old man?' asked Paul.

'Oh, he went down to join the crowd,' said the girl.

'We need a drink,' said Paul, 'got hung up in the middle of it. This is Mrs. Cooper, she cut her arm and lost her shoes. Had a right punch up.'

The girl smiled. 'You always manage to get people involved. Sit down and I'lll get you a beer, it's all we've got.'

'Come on,' said Paul to Linda, 'we'll fix your arm up.' He took her into the bathroom which was surprisingly white and antiseptic-looking. 'So where's Mr. Cooper?' he asked.

Linda looked at him coolly. 'He's away on business.'

'What's your name?'

She hesitated, then said, 'Linda. Why?'

'I just wanted to know.'

They looked at each other and then Linda glanced nervously at the floor. This is ridiculous, she thought. What am I doing here with this boy whom I find so very attractive. What would David think. I must get out.

They discovered a box of Elastoplast and Paul put one over her cut arm. 'Was this your first meeting?'

'Yes,' she replied. 'Look, I simply must get back to my car now; it's really awfully nice of you to have taken all this trouble, but I have people expecting me at home and they will be worried if I'm late.'

'All right,' said Paul. 'I'll take you. Can't have you wandering about London with no shoes on.'

They went back into the large black room. Lank-haired Melanie was sitting clutching a can of beer. She jumped up when Paul came in and rushed over to him. Linda decided she wasn't very pretty, much too thin, and that awful hair!

'Have some beer,' Melanie offered. She had a slightly whiney voice.

'No, we're splitting now,' said Paul, 'I'll be back soon; you wait here.'

The girl obviously wanted to argue but didn't quite dare. Paul kissed the owner of the room. 'Be back.'

Linda said goodbye and they left.

In the street Paul took her arm again but she shook it free. 'I don't like my arm held.'

'What do you like?'

They walked in silence to where Linda had left her car. She felt embarrassed and inelegant in her stockinged feet. Besides that, the pavement was cold and hard and she wished she was safely home.

They reached the car and Paul helped her in. 'Where do you live?' he enquired.

'Finchley. We have a house there.'

'We're neighbours then. I live in Hampstead.' He stood on the pavement leaning against the car door. 'You can drop me back there. Do you mind?'

'I thought you had to go back for your girl-friend,' said Linda nervously. She just wanted to drive off now and leave him standing there. She knew how attracted she was to him, and somehow she felt very vulnerable.

'That's all right, Mel will find her way home. She usually does anyway.' He walked around to the passenger seat and got in.

It's now or never, Linda thought. Either I tell him to get out now or I'm accepting the fact that he's interested and letting him know that I'm interested too. She felt him staring at her. She started the car.

Linda drove expertly through the traffic. Paul sat silently beside her, his silence making her even more aware of his presence. Eventually she spoke. 'You know, your girlfriend isn't going to be too pleased with you, saying you will be back and then just disappearing.'

'It doesn't matter.' They lapsed into silence again. Linda decided that when they reached Hampstead she would stop the car, wait for him to get out, and then wave goodbye and drive quickly away. She would give him no chance to talk about seeing her again, instinctively she knew he would want to.

'I noticed you immediately,' he said.

'What?' she replied, startled.

'I said I noticed you immediately,' he repeated, 'in the crowd. You looked so out of it, so sort of lost. You wanted to be part of it and yet couldn't quite make it. So I grabbed your arm and pulled you into the road and then you were all right, you forgot yourself, y'know?'

'I don't know what you mean,' she said defensively.

'Oh, come off it, you know what I mean, you dig, you're

14

hip. Where's your old man then? Where's your kids? You have got kids, haven't you?'

'Yes, how did you know?'

'It's easy, I could sum you up in a minute. Married maybe ten years, nice little house, mink stole, husband away a lot, kids growing up and leaving you behind. It's true, isn't it?'

Linda's first reaction was one of anger, stop the car and tell this rude little boy to get out, but wait a moment, what he was saying was very near the truth, wait, hear him out, what harm could it do. And then there was curiosity, how did he know? Did she look the part so completely? She forced a smile. 'You're very sure of yourself, aren't you?'

'Yes, I am. I can see it in your face, the way you look, everything about you.'

'We've reached Hampstead,' said Linda quickly. She swerved the little car abruptly into the kerb, 'thanks for the summing up. It was great fun for you, I'm sure. David would have been amused. Goodbye.' She stared straight ahead and waited for him to get out. He didn't move. Eventually he said, 'Can I see you again?' She turned to look at him, his eyes penetrated deep into her own.

'I don't understand you. First you dissect my life, pull me to pieces and then you ask to see me again. No, you can't. I'm in love with my husband. I have two lovely children and I live a very nice life, thank you. I think you are a very rude boy, and do you mind getting out of my car and going away.'

'I would like to see you again. I think you need someone like me.' He opened the car door and got out. 'Anyway, if you change your mind, I'm around.' He turned and walked away.

Linda watched him go. He's a hippy, she thought angrily. He's very thin, probably never eats. So young, but so knowing. I would like to sleep with him. She halted her train of thought abruptly. I would like to what? she asked herself incredulously. Sex had always been synonymous with David. She had never had an affair, she had gone to her marriage bed a virgin, and now this thought was in her head. Oh, there had been many boys she had dated, necked with, before getting married, but never anything more serious than that. David is a' wonderful husband, she thought, a wonderful lover. But when did he ever make

15

love to her these days? Maybe once a fortnight, and then it was a quick ten minute affair, out of which she derived no particular pleasure, and afterwards he would turn over and go straight to sleep and snore, and she would lie awake for a long time thinking how it used to be before the children, when they were first married. She sighed and started the car, it was impossible to turn the clock back.

The house was empty, even the dogs were away with the children and their live-in Spanish maid, Anna, was out for the day. It was depressing. Linda switched the television on in the bedroom. It was nearly six; David had said he would be home around nine, so there were three hours to kill. She had no intention of watching the television, but it was nice to have human voices around her. She decided to 'phone her mother and see how Jane and Stephen were behaving themselves. She dialled the operator who put her through. Her mother's voice, placid and comfortable, came on to the line. 'Hello, Linda, is that you, dear?'

'Hello, mother, how's everything?'

'Oh, fine dear, fine. Jane's having her bath now and Stephen's right here. Wait a minute, hang on, he wants to speak to you.'

There was a pause and then Stephen's thin excitable voice came on the line. He was eight. 'Hello, Mummy. We're having a smashing time. Grandma made lots of gooey cakes for tea and that pig Jane tried to eat them all so I pushed her off her chair and she started to cry and . . .' He carried on at geat length about the cakes and then her mother's voice came back on the line.

'Daddy will be driving the children back after lunch tomorrow, so you should expect them about four. How is David? Did you have a nice peaceful week-end together?'

'Yes, Mother, very peaceful,' replied Linda ruefully. 'All right, then, I will speak to you later in the week. Thanks for having the children, kiss Janey for me. 'Bye.'

What now? Feeling slightly hungry she went to the kitchen, but she hated cooking just for herself, so she finally settled for a cheese sandwich. There seemed nothing else left to do except go to bed and wait for David. Bed, David, the two thoughts connected in her head, and a sudden idea formed. She rushed to her wardrobe and hunted around until she found what she was looking for. A long slinky black

16

négligée she had bought in Paris several years ago and never really got around to wearing. It had always seemed too frivolous. She held it up against her, and then returned to the kitchen to iron it. Well, this is what they say in all the women's magazines, she thought, smiling, shock your husband into realizing how utterly sexy and devastating you really are!

After the négligée was ironed, she ran a long hot bath and borrowed some of Janey's Baby Bubbles to throw in. For good measure she added some Chanel No. 5 cologne and the whole thing looked very luxurious and inviting. Next she creamed her face, set her hair, and then climbed into the bath and relaxed. The 'phone rang. Wrapped in a bath towel, trailing bubbles, she hurried into the bedroom to answer it.

'Hello.'

'Hello, Linda.'

'Yes.'

'This is Paul Bedford.'

A long silence, and then his voice again. 'You mentioned David and Finchley, so it was easy to trace you in the 'phone book. Look, I'm sorry, I wanted to apologize for earlier. I didn't mean to be so rude. Will you forgive me?'

'There is nothing to forgive,' said Linda coolly. 'It certainly didn't bother me one way or the other.' She was tempted to say goodbye and hang up, but she waited to see what he would say next.

'Oh well, that's all right then.' He sounded relieved. 'You know, when I like people, I mean really like them, I always seem to rub them up the wrong way. I don't intend to, but it just happens. Sort of reverse action, I suppose.' He paused, then continued. 'Listen, a friend of mine is having a party tonight, he lives near you, and I thought you might like to come.'

'I'm sorry I can't,' she answered quickly.

'Well, no harm in trying. Maybe some other time.'

'You will have to excuse me, I'm in the middle of taking a bath.' She paused, and then added, 'thanks for the thought anyway. Goodbye, Paul.'

'Goodbye, Linda. Sorry about dragging you out of the bath. The party doesn't start till after ten, so if you should decide you would like to go, my number is Hampstead

17

09911. 'Bye.' He hung up.

O-double-nine-double-one, so easy to remember. She shivered and made her way quickly back to the bathroom. The bubbles in the bath had gone flat and the water when she got back in was lukewarm. She was secretly pleased that Paul had 'phoned, it made her feel desirable and wanted, a feeling she couldn't remember having had for a long time. Tonight things would be different, she would make David realize that everything could and should be as romantic as it was when they first knew each other. After all, just because two people were married didn't mean that romance had to go by the board. She sang softly to herself. I'm only thirty-three, she thought, that's still very young, well certainly not old. She climbed out of the bath, and studied her naked body in the bathroom mirror. I could do with going on a diet, she mused. Her legs were shapely but a little heavy around the thighs, her waist was quite slim and her breasts, although large and full, were still firm. She slipped into the négligée. It clung flatteringly and she was pleased with the effect. She applied a light make-up and combed out her hair. Then she went down to the lounge and fetched the portable gramophone, taking it to the bedroom. She searched around and found some old Nat King Cole albums and put them on, his dreamy voice was much more acceptable than the noise of the television, which she had switched off.

The stage was set, the player was ready, it was nearly nine. A little glass of wine would be nice, she thought. There was a bottle of rosé in the fridge, so she went and got it.

An hour passed. The wine was drunk, the records had come to a stop, the black négligée had been replaced with something a little warmer. The television was back on and Linda huddled morosely in front of it, watching an American crime serial.

She was a little loaded. The emptiness of the house seemed to press around her. Where was David? He had said nine o'clock. If he was going to be late, he could at least 'phone. He was usually very prompt, it was one of his better habits. Perhaps he had had a car accident. Perhaps he was lying badly injured or even ...

The 'phone rang. First, the operator's cool efficient voice, and then David, obviously in a hurry. 'Look, I'm held up with these people here. I had to drive over from Leeds to Manchester, and I'm bushed. Not going to risk driving back

18

tonight, it's a filthy night. I'll leave early in the morning and be home about eight.'

'But, David, I'm expecting you,' she tried to keep her voice pleasant. 'Why couldn't you have let me know earlier, it's nearly ten, and you promised to be home by nine.'

'Look. I can't talk now, I'll explain tomorrow.'

Her temper suddenly snapped. 'I don't care about tomorrow. What about me? I've had a bloody miserable week-end and tonight I've just sat around waiting for you, and you couldn't even bother to 'phone. At least if I'd known I could have gone to the films or something. You're just selfish, and I can't . . .'

His voice was cold and unemotional, 'I'm with people now, I'll see you tomorrow. Goodbye.'

The line went dead in Linda's hand and she sat very still trying to control a choking feeling of complete frustration. He had hung up on her, he hadn't even bothered to wait for her to say goodbye. At last she replaced the receiver, only to pick it up again and dial. The ringing tone seemed very loud in her ear. I've had too much to drink, she thought vaguely, then a voice was saying hello and she found herself replying with, 'Hello, Paul, this is Linda. About that party . . .'

CHAPTER THREE

It was four o'clock when David and Claudia arrived back at her flat. She lived in a converted house at the back of Knightsbridge. It had been made into six flats and was all very new and modern. She occupied the top flat which had the advantage of having a small roof garden. David had often found himself wondering how she could afford it. All her furniture was new and obviously expensive and she had an enormous wardrobe of clothes.

She was an actress and model and from what David knew

of both professions unless you were extremely successful you didn't earn an awful lot of money. Certainly not enough to keep Claudia in the style she was living. He had mulled this problem over in his mind and come to no real satisfactory conclusion. Eventually, he had decided that she must have a rich father, although this didn't really tie in with the bits and pieces he knew of her background.

She had left home at fifteen and come to London, and now she was twenty and had ambitions to be a successful film actress. She was very beautiful and sparkled like champagne. He had known her only three weeks, and in that time seen her as much as twelve times. She had always been free to see him; there didn't appear to be any other man in the picture. She accepted the situation that he was a married man, and didn't nag about it as a lot of women might. She had never mentioned money to him. He had seen that she did the Beauty Maid commercial, but apart from that she didn't appear to have worked at all. David decided that he must find out more about her; maybe she needed money and was embarrassed to mention it. He resolved to bring the subject up.

When they entered, Claudia rushed about making a great show of fixing the bed and generally tidying up. She was most undomesticated and had a daily woman who came in except for week-ends. She made a disgusted 'ugh' when she came to the dirty dishes in the kitchen. David followed her in. 'I'll buy you a dishwashing machine,' he said, slipping his arms around her waist.

She turned laughing. 'You're joking, of course. A dishwashing machine! What a terrible present. I'll have something more romantic than that, thank you!'

'What do you want? We'll go shopping tomorrow.'

'I want, let me see now, I want a Ferrari, two mink coats, lots of diamonds, a beautiful penthouse in New York, and a villa on the Riviera!' She started to laugh. 'Can you afford me?'

'I'm serious. Will you settle for a mink jacket? Go and order it tomorrow.'

Claudia looked at him. 'You really are serious. Baby, that's fabulous, I would adore that. But if you want me to have it, surprise me, none of this ordering jazz; I like surprises.'

'All right, a surprise it will be.' He wondered if now was
20

the time to bring up her financial situation, and decided against it. Later, when they were in bed.

'What time do you have to turn into Cinderella tonight?' asked Claudia.

'I should leave about eight thirty,' he stroked her hair, 'but I can always stretch a point, depending on what the main attraction is.'

She giggled and suddenly pulled off her sweater. 'The second feature is starting now. The main attraction should prove to be very interesting indeed!'

Sometime later when David looked at his watch, he was surprised to find it was well after nine. Claudia lay asleep beside him, her long hair in disarray around her face, her make-up smudged and faded. She looked very young. Her clothes were scattered around the bedroom, leading in a trail from the kitchen. As if she sensed him looking at her, she opened her eyes, yawned and stretched and made contented noises.

'You're like a cat,' he said, 'sometimes an innocent little kitten and sometimes the wildest dirtiest alley cat around.'

'I like that. I can see myself telling it to someone in the years to come. There was this guy and he said to me, you're like a cat, sometimes . . .'

He put his hand over her mouth. 'Don't say that. There will be no other guys in the years to come, only me. I love you and I want to marry you.' He was surprised himself to hear the words, but there they were, spoken aloud for all to hear.

'You know, it's amazing,' she said, 'how very easy it is for married men to propose. I guess it's an easy thing for them to say, because really they are all safe and secure, and they know they can lay out this tasty bit of bait without a hope in hell of getting trapped themselves. Marry me, my darling, only don't let my wife find out!

David was furious. So all right, he hadn't really meant it. Correction, he had meant it but, as she said, was secure in the knowledge that it was not possible. However, the fact that Claudia realized this infuriated him. Why did women always seem to have so much insight into the things men said? 'I could get a divorce,' he said.

'Are you going to?' replied Claudia.

'I don't know,' he pulled her to him, 'it's not just me and

21

Linda; there are the children to consider. But I love you, and I want to look after you, and one day when my kids are a bit older, well then everything will work itself out. I don't want you to be in that rat race you're in. I can look after you, and you needn't do anything. I don't want you to work.'

She stared up at him with her large slanty green eyes. 'Well, I'm glad you have it all figured out.' She caressed his back, and he felt desire rise up in him again. She had only to touch him and he wanted her. 'There is only one problem. I don't want to marry you. Not even if you were free, and we could rush off and do it now.' She wriggled away from him and got off the bed. She stood looking at him, completely naked, and continued, 'I want to do what I want to do whenever I want. No ties, no strings. I don't dig this marriage bit, it means nothing to me, so don't offer it like it's the golden hoop, because I'm just not going to jump. I love you now, today, but tomorrow who knows? That's me, I don't make any pretence to be something I'm not, so why don't you do the same?'

He couldn't control the choking excitement he felt for her as she stood there; her words didn't matter. He dragged her back on the bed, and let loose his fury and frustrations on her. She tried to struggle but he crushed her beneath him, until her struggling stopped and became part of him.

For David it was devastating; with Claudia it always was. She was unlike any other woman he had ever known. And each time it was more, both emotionally and physically.

'You had better get up, it's past the witching hour and wifey will be waiting.'

'Don't be a bitch; anyway, I think I'll stay.'

She kissed him. They 'phoned Linda, and Claudia pretended to be the operator so that the call appeared to be coming long distance.

Afterwards, she said, 'No son of a bitch would talk to me that way and get away with it. I feel sorry for your wife.'

'Do you?' he said shortly. It annoyed him when Claudia discussed Linda.

'Yes, I do, although it's her own fault.'

'What do you mean?'

'Well, darling. I mean really, what made me more exciting to you than her? Because I was new and younger and prettier. Am I prettier?'

22

'Yes, you're prettier.'

'But you shouldn't have to look around. She should be new to you, she should make bloody sure that she's always new to you. Most women seem to get married and then stop trying. Well, we've caught the fish, now put away the bait and only bring it out on special occasions. I'm not saying that you wouldn't screw around once in a while, all men do, even the happiest of married men. But that's all it would be, there would be no affairs like me, you wouldn't need them.'

'Thank you, marriage councillor Parker, but I have a feeling that you are addressing the wrong party.'

'Shall I speak to your wife? What shall I say? Darling, in strict confidence I'm banging your husband. This isn't really necessary, if only you weren't so dullsville he might fancy you again. Liven up a bit, and back he will come.'

They both started to laugh. 'You are a bitch. Is that why I love you?'

'No,' she giggled, 'you know why you love me.'

They got up and Claudia busied herself in the kitchen making sandwiches while David prowled around the flat thinking how he could bring up the subject of her finances. She had annoyed him with her little speech about not wanting to marry him. But really he wasn't too annoyed, because on thinking it over he decided she had only said it as a defence mechanism. She knew they couldn't get married, so to save face she had probably convinced herself that she didn't want marriage anyway. On thinking it over even further, he became almost pleased about it, because it put him in the enviable position of being able to have his cake and eat it too.

He didn't really want to leave Linda; in his own way he loved her, although she had ceased to attract him sexually shortly after they were married. He had compensated for this by different affairs throughout the years, and to Linda he had been more than generous materially. She was the perfect wife figure. A lovely hostess and mother. No, he certainly didn't want to leave Linda. He felt no particular guilt about being unfaithful to her, although if the shoe had been on the other foot, so to speak, but no, that was unthinkable: the very idea of Linda being unfaithful to him was ridiculous.

Claudia was licking mayonnaise off her fingers in the

kitchen. She was wearing a pink kimono and had tied her hair away from her face.

'You look about fifteen,' he said.

'And you look about fifty. What *is* on your mind? Are you brooding because I turned down your gallant proposal?'

'I want to talk to you seriously. Bring the sandwiches and come and sit down.'

She followed him into the living-room and, munching a sandwich, she sat down on the floor near his feet. 'Now isn't this cosy, so what seems to be bothering you?'

'Look darling, I've been thinking a lot about you.'

She giggled. 'I should hope so.'

'This is serious, Claudia,' he continued. 'I've been worried about you, about how you manage financially. I mean, well this flat isn't cheap and I want to help you out. I mean, well frankly, where do you get your money?'

Claudia sat very still, her eyes glinted dangerously. However, she managed to keep her voice pleasant. 'Well, baby,' she said sweetly, 'what makes you want to know?'

David didn't observe the danger signals. 'Of course I want to know. Do you get an allowance from your father or what?'

'Oh, come on, I haven't seen my family for five years and I don't care if I never see them again. My old man wouldn't give me a penny to go to the bathroom with.' She sat silently then, and David realized that she had no intention of answering him.

'Claudia, I want to know.'

She arose. 'I don't like being questioned. I'm not asking you for anything. I don't want anything from you.' She started to shout, 'leave me alone with your questions. What's on your mind? Where do you think I get money from? Do you think I'm a whore? Well, if I was, wouldn't I be asking you for money?' She was crying and David was shocked that he had provoked such anger. 'It's my business where I get my money from and if you don't like the idea of that then let's just forget it.'

David had caught her mood of fury by this time. 'All right,' he said coldly, 'we'll forget it.' He marched into the bedroom and dressed. Claudia didn't follow him. When he came out she was sitting on the sofa reading a magazine. She didn't look up.

He stood there, undecided about whether to walk out or not. 'Well, are you going to tell me?'

She continued reading and didn't answer him.

'Goodbye' he said, and left.

In the hall outside her front door he immediately regretted this move. He couldn't go home and he debated making it up with Claudia, but that was impossible. If he gave way to her now he would be admitting defeat and he never admitted defeat to any woman. No, he decided to let her stew a little and she would come running back, they always did.

He went downstairs to his car, having decided to spend the night in a Turkish bath. He was puzzled why Claudia was so secretive about the source of her income; it could only mean that it was something he wouldn't like. Well, in that case, when she told him he would stop it, whatever it was, and then she would be dependent on him, which was exactly the way he wanted it.

He drove to the Turkish baths in Jermyn Street, and, after going through the hot and cold steam baths and having a massage, he was quite happy to settle down in his small white cubicle, where he promptly fell asleep. Tomorrow he would settle everything.

CHAPTER FOUR

Paul looked younger than Linda remembered him. He was wearing a black sweater and tight black trousers. She had decided to wear a plain dark blue cocktail dress after discarding several other outfits. They met at a pre-arranged spot and Paul helped her out of her car and said he would drive as he knew the way.

'I'm glad you changed your mind. What did it? My irresistible charm?'

'I don't know.' All the wine she had drunk and the rushing to get ready had finally made her tired. 'Maybe I shouldn't have come. I don't know why I'm here really.'

He looked at her. 'I'm glad you're here. I don't think you will be sorry you came. In fact I promise you that.'

They drove a short way along the Heath and Paul eventually pulled into the drive of an old rambling house. Its windows were ablaze with lights and the belting voice of Solomon Burke screamed out. A couple were arguing in the open doorway and, as they arrived several more people came pushing through the door with much laughter and yelling. Paul parked the car and they went in.

The scene that greeted their eyes was somewhat wild to say the least. The front door led into a small hall with big rooms off either side of it and a large staircase in the centre. The staircase was littered with various people, a lot of men with beards, girls sitting and standing, and everyone steadily drinking. The room on the right was filled with dancing couples, moving, or just standing and necking. There appeared to be no furniture, only a rather battered old record player balanced precariously on the window sill. The room on the left featured a thin girl with stringy red hair taking off her clothes to the beat of some bongos being hammered on by a West Indian clad only in white slacks. No one was taking much notice of them, mostly people were watching a blond boy at the other end of the room who was standing on a chair stark naked reciting an obscene poem.

Paul squeezed Linda's arm. 'Come on,' he said, leading her up the stairs and greeting people as he went. 'Let's get rid of your coat and then we can get a drink.'

Upstairs there were more rooms which seemed equally devoid of furniture. Paul steered her into a room with a bed creaking under the weight of many coats. Two girls were staring deep into each other's eyes in a corner, and another girl was either asleep or had passed out at the bottom of the bed. Linda took off her coat and felt too dressed-up in her neat cocktail dress. Paul said that she looked great and took her to find a drink. They went downstairs to the room on the left. The redhead had abandoned her strip and was sitting on the floor, someone's sweater covering her. She grabbed hold of Paul's leg as he went by. 'You look sexy, want to make it?' Her voice was slurred. 'I've got a great body.'

Linda found herself separated from Paul and she headed towards a table where the drinks appeared to be coming from. A fat man pounced up behind her. 'You look very smart,' he said, 'who are you?' His face was beaded with sweat and his breath was a combination of onions and stale beer. 'Do you want a drink?'

'Yes, please,' said Linda, trying to edge away from the full blast of his breath.

He poured her a very large scotch in a cracked glass and she drank it down hastily. 'Let us go and dance,' he said, and put his arm around her waist. She could feel the hotness of his hand penetrate her dress through to her skin.

'Not just now,' she said, trying to disentangle herself from him.

He licked his pudgy lips and then Paul arrived. 'Hello, Bruno, I see you've met Linda.'

The fat man removed his arm. 'Oh, she's yours, is she?' he said hastily. 'I don't know what they see in you.' He wiped his mouth with a plump pink hand and ambled away.

Paul laughed. 'Don't take any notice of him,' he said, and then was suddenly serious. 'You're very lovely.' He took hold of her hand.

'Oh,' said Linda. She had never been able to accept compliments easily.

She drained her glass. 'I'd like another drink.'

Paul poured her another large scotch and she drank it quickly, feeling its burning effect almost immediately. 'I think I should go home,' she said weakly, 'I'm a little bit drunk, you know.'

'I know.' He pushed her towards the wall and then he leaned forward and kissed her. She closed her eyes and felt the intimacy of his tongue penetrate her lips. His mouth was persistent and demanding. She felt she should push him away but didn't have the strength and anyway she didn't want to. It was a long time since she had been kissed like this. David never kissed her any more and she had forgotten how exciting a kiss could be.

'Oh, so here you are,' the whiney voice was familiar and the note of anger was unmistakable. Paul straightened up. Melanie was standing there, her yellow hair hanging in a straight curtain around her thin flushed face. 'I thought you were coming back for me.' She glared at Linda. 'Or have you been so busy that you couldn't find time.'

'Oh, I'm sorry, Mel, thought I'd see you here.'

'Well, you didn't.' Her voice was becoming almost shrill. 'And how's Mrs. Cooper? Recovered I see.'

'Can it, Mel,' said Paul sharply. He steered her away from Linda and into the hall. 'Look, I'm sorry, but that's the way it is.'

'That's the way what is?' Suddenly her eyes filled with tears.

'Look, Mel, it's been great, but we've been heading this way a long time now, and I think that it's best to forget it. I still dig you and all that bit, but, well you know ...'

'No, I don't know. And anyway, what can you see in that old bag in there.' She started to cry. 'I hate you, Paul.'

'Look, kid, you're seventeen, there will be lots of other guys, you'll soon forget me. We're just not ...'

'We're not what?' she interrupted angrily. 'I think you're rotten and I hate you.'

He shrugged and walked away. Linda was deep in conversation with the fat man again. 'Do you want to go?' Paul asked her.

'No.' Her eyes were bright, she was very drunk. Bruno's going to teach me to shake.'

'Bruno can find a girl-friend of his own. I'll teach you.' He took her into the other room where the dancing was going on, and then he held her very tight. 'I want to sleep with you,' he whispered.

'I want to sleep with you too,' she whispered back. 'I mean I don't want to, but it would be nice, but I ... Oh, God, I think I had better get some air.'

He kissed her again. This time she kissed him back and their mouths met in mutual enjoyment. They stood still amongst the dancers, lost in their own little world. His tongue explored her mouth and she felt a sudden hot desire for him. He pressed her very close, and then released her.

'You wait here,' he said. 'I'll get your coat.'

She stood patiently waiting, the liquor she had drunk falling over her in waves. She couldn't think clearly at all, her head buzzed and she wanted to be back again in the safety of Paul's arms. There was a lot of noise coming from the hall and she wandered out there. Two men were fighting. It was the fat man, Bruno, and the West Indian who had been playing the bongos earlier. They screamed obscenities at each other, and rolled about on the floor. No one tried to stop them.

'Why are they fighting?' Linda asked a girl standing near her.

28

'Oh, darling, Bruno always has to fight with someone,' the girl said, 'it wouldn't be Bruno if he didn't.'

The West Indian's nose had started to bleed and there was a lot of blood. Linda suddenly felt very sick. She edged her way to the front door and got out. The cold air had a slightly sobering effect. She went over to the car and sat in it.

Eventually Paul arrived. 'I was worried, I thought you had walked out on me.' He got in the car and put his arm around her. She pulled away. 'What's the matter?' he continued.

'I feel terrible. I think I'm going to be sick.'

'Oh great, let's get back inside and I'll get you upstairs to the bathroom.'

'No, I don't want to go back in there.'

'You'll feel better in a minute.' He put his arm around her again and this time she didn't pull away. He kissed her and his hands started to explore her body. She felt weak and her head spun, and when she shut her eyes everything whirled round and round. She could feel Paul touching her and his mouth on hers, but it all seemed like it was happening to someone else.

Abruptly he let go of her and started the car, and they seemed to be driving for ages, but really it was no time at all. Then he was helping her out of the car and they were climbing a lot of stairs, and then they were in a room, and he was pushing her on to a bed. She didn't struggle when he unzipped her dress and pulled it off because, after all, this wasn't really her that this was happening to. He kissed her slowly and the bed was very soft and she felt very comfortable. His arms were strong and warm, and his hands created a fantastic excitement in her. He rolled her over on her stomach and she felt him undoing the hooks on her strapless bra.

'I'm not here,' she whispered, 'I'm on another planet. I'm very drunk, you shouldn't take disadvantage of me, I'm at an advantage . . .' She started to giggle.

He began to kiss her back, and then she was suddenly lost in a raging enveloping holocaust of love, which seemed to go on for ever and ever.

'I love you,' one of them said.

'I love you,' the other said.

Linda awoke about five a.m. She opened her eyes in disbelief. She felt parched with an awful thirst. Her eyes felt heavy and her face like sandpaper. She looked around her. She was in a small untidy room, and Paul was sprawled across the end of the bed asleep.

She sat up slowly and looked around for something to cover herself. Her head felt it would split open if she moved too rapidly. She pulled a cover off the bed and, wrapping it round her, she got up. Paul didn't stir. She groped her way to the door and found herself in a tiny hallway piled high with clutter. She made her way through to the bathroom which was a small dusty room with everything rusting and old. She switched on the light; it was a naked bulb, and then she turned on the cold water tap. A large black spider ran disdainfully across the basin and she almost screamed. She found a tooth-mug and quickly drank four mugfuls of water. It tasted faintly of toothpaste but made her feel a little better in spite of that. She stared in the mirror above the basin. Her make-up was smeared and etched into deep lines about her face. Her hair was untidy and matted. I look like I belong here, she thought vaguely.

She padded back into the bedroom and searched for her clothes. When she found them she dressed quickly. She looked at Paul. He slept deeply. She stared at him for a long time and then, finding her coat, she left.

It was cold and silent in the street. Her car coughed and spluttered and she thought that it would never start. At last it did, and she drove home through the deserted streets.

She let herself quietly into the house and went straight to her bedroom. Everything looked clean and new. She took a hot bath and then collapsed into bed, where she lay and thought. She couldn't exactly remember what she had done or what had happened between her and Paul. But obviously she had slept with him.

She felt a tremendous feeling of guilt and also a certain horror at herself for having allowed it to happen. Yes, she had been drunk, but was that any real excuse?

At last she fell asleep, knowing that in the morning she would have to face herself and David. For Linda this wasn't a pleasant thought.

She tossed and turned and slept restlessly.

CHAPTER FIVE

David left the Turkish baths at eight in the morning. He felt refreshed and invigorated. He had contemplated phoning Claudia, but had then decided to wait the day out and see if she called him. He parked his car, and bought the morning papers, and then made his way along Piccadilly to Lyons where he planned to breakfast before continuing on home.

He ordered bacon and eggs, toast and coffee, and then sat back to scan the papers. His eye was immediately caught by a half page picture on the front page of the *Daily Mirror*. It was captioned More Near-Riots in Trafalgar Square, and the picture was of an angry mob of people surrounding two policemen in the process of carrying a woman away from the road, and obviously about to dump her back on the pavement. The woman's skirt was high above her waist. Her hair was flopping over her face, and one shoe was about to fall from her struggling foot. It was an effective picture.

The waitress arrived with the order. She was plump and Cockney. She peered over his shoulder at the paper. ''Ere what does she think she looks like,' she muttered, 'about time all this rubbish was stopped. A load of show-offs, that's all they are. They should lock the lot of 'em up!' She wandered away, cluck-clucking about nothing in particular. David was staring at the photo, horrified. The woman was unmistakably Linda. He shook his head in disbelief. What was she doing? What was she thinking of?

He gulped his coffee, scalded his tongue, swore, found himself unable to eat anything and called for the bill.

The waitress padded slowly back. 'What's the matter, dear? Isn't everything all right?'

He thrust a pound note at her. 'Everything's fine,' he said, and stormed out.

A parking warden was in attendance beside his car. David brushed impatiently past him. 'I'm afraid you'll have to wait while I finish writing out this ticket, sir,' said the warden. 'I suppose you are aware that this is a restricted zone for parking?'

'Just give me the ticket and get on with it,' said David brusquely.

The warden glared at him, and then proceeded to take his time.

David drove away, his face grim. He envisaged what he would say to Linda. He couldn't quite make up his mind what he would say. The whole thing was so utterly ridiculous. His wife, at a protest meeting! It was ludicrous. She didn't know anything about politics or bombs. The kitchen and the children and social activities such as tea with the girls and dinner out twice a week were her province. Ban the Bomb indeed! Who did she think she was? Claudia was forgotten. He put his foot hard down on the acclerator and raced home.

Anna let him in. 'Mrs. Cooper, she slept late,' she announced. 'You like tea?'

'No,' he grunted, already halfway up the stairs to the bedroom. Linda was asleep, curled up and buried beneath the covers. He drew the curtains, throwing glaring daylight into the room. Linda didn't stir. He paced the floor, coughed loudly and, when she still didn't appear to show any signs of waking up, he went over and shook her roughly, thrusting a copy of the *Daily Mirror* in front of her face as she sleepily opened her eyes.

'What's all this about?' he demanded angrily.

A feeling of dread ran through her. He had found out about her and Paul! How! So soon. She sat up quickly. David stood there glowering at her. He continued talking, 'What is this then? Some secret ambition of yours to make yourself look a complete fool?' He brandished the paper at her again, and she took it from him. A feeling of relief passed over her when she realized that this was what he was so furious about.

'What an awful photo!' she exclaimed. 'I didn't know they were taking any photos.'

'Is that all you have to say?' He mimicked her, 'I didn't know they were taking any photos.' He snatched the paper away from her and continued in a loud angry voice. 'What were you doing there anyway? What were you thinking of?'

'I had nothing else to do. I just found myself there. I'm sorry that you're so angry about it.'

'I'm not angry,' he screamed. He always screamed when in a temper. 'I like to see photos of my wife smeared all

32

over the papers, with her skirt around her waist, accompanied by a load of scruffs.'

She got out of bed. 'I'm not going to sit here while you yell at me. Perhaps if you spent a week-end at home for a change this might not have happened.'

Just then the telephone rang. Linda suddenly felt very hot and flushed. Supposing it was Paul? Should she answer it, or would it be best to let David pick it up and then maybe Paul would hang up. She was convinced it was him.

David swooped on it, and barked into the receiver. 'Hello.'

Linda held her breath, and then David launched into a long conversation with someone from his office.

She took advantage of his preoccupation on the 'phone and dressed. When he had finished talking he seemed a little calmer. 'Do you want some breakfast?' she asked him.

'No. I have to make some calls. There's this party tonight to launch the Beauty Maid soap product; I had forgotten all about it. You had better meet me at the office at seven, and we'll go from there. I hope to Christ nobody has noticed all your publicity.'

She groaned inwardly at the thought of another party, and then mentally planned her day, which included being at home to greet the children and a definite visit to the hairdressers.

David meanwhile had his own thoughts. Claudia would most certainly be at the party; she was being paid to be there. He wondered if it would be possible for him to effect a quiet reconciliation without everyone in the room noticing. He must be sure that Linda didn't become suspicious, she seemed to be getting a little too concerned about him being away so much. Maybe she was beginning to suspect him, although this seemed unlikely as he had managed to get away with various affairs throughout the years and she had never found him out yet. At least he would be able to see Claudia. He started to make his business calls.

The children burst back into the house at exactly four o'clock. Linda's father was always prompt. She had just returned from the hairdressers and Stephen flung his small wiry body at her, practically knocking her down.

'We've had a smashing time, Mummy,' he exclaimed.

'I'm starving. What have we got for tea? Grandma makes lovely cakes!'

His sister Jane gave Linda a small kiss. She was six and rather shy. 'I'm glad we're home, Mummy. Your hair looks all pretty, are you and Daddy going out?'

Linda greeted her father and then they sat and chatted while Anna served tea and the children rushed around rediscovering their various toys.

Linda was only half listening as her father droned on about Stephen and Jane's activities during the week-end. She thought about Paul. What did he think of her? Why hadn't he telephoned? What would she say if he phoned and David was there?

Finally her father left and the children were settled with Anna having their dinner; and then she got herself ready. Just as she was about to leave the house the telephone rang. She so expected it to be Paul that she felt herself break out in a sweat and her hand started to shake as she picked up the receiver. 'Hello.'

'Hello, darling, it's Monica. How about *you*, then! Aren't *you* the dark horse! Fancy leaving us yesterday and not saying a word about where you were going. You are a deep one. What does David think about it all?'

'Oh,' replied Linda, 'he's not too pleased.'

Monica laughed. 'Well, darling, not to worry. Jack and I think it's marvellous. Anyway, sweetie, we're having a few people over after dinner tonight and we should love you and David to come.'

'Well, Monica, we have to go to a sort of a press party launching the new soap product tonight, and I don't know what time we will be able to get away.'

'Never mind, darling, just come along when you've finished. You know us, we're *always* late.' She gave Linda no chance to protest. 'See you later then, 'bye darling.'

Linda replaced the receiver. She really wasn't too fond of Monica and Jack and she certainly didn't feel like seeing them later. However, she would have to tell David as he would probably want to go.

She left the house in a bad mood. She had a headache, and she was half angry and half relieved that Paul hadn't phoned her. She desperately wanted him to phone, otherwise what had it all been? A quick one-night affair, a meeting of two people with no more in common than a few hours in bed. However, if he did 'phone, she wanted to tell him that she couldn't possibly see him again, that it could lead nowhere, and that it had all been a mistake. She sighed, at least that way she would be regaining a small amount of self-respect, by denying herself something she really wanted.

It was all so unexpected. She had really never thought of herself as the sort of woman who could have an affair. And this boy Paul, he was so much younger than her, and so different from the type of people she knew and mixed with. How had it happened? She searched her mind and finally concluded that it must be a failure on her part to have reached a complete fulfilment in her marriage. She resolved to try and put the episode with Paul out of her mind and to work desperately and make things more satisfactory between herself and David.

It was nine o'clock before Claudia appeared at the Beauty Maid soap party. David had been watching for her all evening, and suddenly there she was. She materialized beside him, looking exceptionally beautiful, and she murmured, 'Good evening, Mr. Cooper.'

David was taken off guard. He was standing talking to a group which included several press boys and their wives, and Linda. He was flustered and Claudia smiled faintly. The group of people were looking expectantly at him, waiting to be introduced. At last he said, 'Oh, this is Claudia Parker, our Beauty Maid girl.'

Claudia smiled round at the group. She was very flushed and her eyes shone. David knew at once that she was a little loaded. She wore an orange dress, dangerously low cut, and the women in the gathering found themselves standing up straighter and throwing out their bosoms, as if in answer to this sudden challenge. The men were all obviously impressed. 'Miss Parker,' Ned Rice, a small beady-eyed reporter, pressed closer towards her. 'What do you really think of Beauty Maid soap?' His eyes darted towards her bosom.

Claudia played up to him; she fluttered her very long eyelashes and gave him one of her deep sexy looks. 'Well,' she said at last, 'actually I'm an actress really, therefore I don't feel I can give you a serious opinion on soap! As a matter of fact, I've just come from seeing Conrad Lee and he's very interested in having me in his new picture.' She shot David a triumphant look.

Ned Rice was most interested. 'That sounds wonderful. Perhaps we could do a piece about you on our film page.'

'Yes, that would be lovely,' Claudia smiled. 'I'll give you my 'phone number.'

David suddenly could stand it no more. He gripped her by the arm, smiled tightly and said, 'I hope you will excuse us, Miss Parker is here for a purpose, she will be demonstrating our product and I think she's due to begin pretty soon, so I had better get her over to Phillip Abbottson.'

'Oh well, Miss Parker,' said Ned Rice, 'I'll see you later and we'll get together on this.'

'Yes, fine,' she gave one last radiant smile around the group and then followed David.

As soon as they were out of earshot he exploded. 'You're drunk,' he accused, 'where have you been? You were supposed to be here by eight.'

She gave him a cool look. 'David baby, you're nothing in my life, so why don't you just leave me alone.'

'You bitch,' he said in a low voice, his grip tightened on her arm.

'I'm going to make a scene if you don't let go of me,' she said quietly, 'I'm tired of you telling me what I should do. I'm not someone's wife who has to answer questions and account for every second of her life.'

At that moment, Phillip Abbottson rushed up to them.

'What *is* going on?' he asked. 'Claudia, you were supposed to be here an hour ago. We're waiting to unveil the display, get changed for Christ's sake, you think we want to be here all night?' He gave David an odd look and then with Claudia in tow rushed off again.

Ned Rice sidled up to David. His plump pasty wife was talking to Linda across the other side of the room. 'Quite a bit, your Miss Parker,' he said with a leer, 'I bet she's a hot little number, a real tiger!'

David endeavoured to remain calm. 'I wouldn't know.'

'Oh well then, in that case I expect it's all right for me to have a bash.' He nudged David. 'These starlets are all the same, y'know. You've jost got to tell them you can get their name in print and they pull their drawers down without you even asking!'

David was saved from answering by the arrival of Mrs. Rice and Linda from across the room.

Ned affectionately patted his wife's plump shoulder. 'Enjoying yourself, love?' he asked, then he waggled an accusing finger at Linda. 'And what were you up to making front page news this morning?'

David was beginning to dislike Ned Rice more and more.

Just then, the lights in the room were dimmed and a spotlight was focused on the mock stage, set at one end of the room. Phillip Abbottson was standing poised at a microphone, and as soon as the hubbub of chatter died down he launched into a long speech about Beauty Maid soap. He was a good promoter and made a simple bar of soap sound like a solid block of gold. At the end of his speech there was polite scattered applause and then he stood to one side and said, 'And now I would like to introduce you to Miss Beauty Maid herself!'

The curtains were drawn back, and there sat Claudia, in a marble bath surrounded by bubbles, in fact an exact replica of the set that was used in the television commercial. She was wearing her flesh-coloured swimsuit, but of course no one could see it, so the general assumption was that she had nothing on beneath the bubbles.

David felt a surge of excitement. Claudia smiled at her audience and started to recite her Beauty Maid speech. Ned Rice whispered something obscene in David's ear. Mrs. Rice said to Linda, 'Isn't she a pretty little thing.' Linda stared blankly into space, her thoughts on the night before.

When Claudia finished talking there was hearty applause from the men and a few jealous titters from the women. Then the curtains were drawn on Claudia and Phillip appeared back at the microphone with more to say.

David excused himself from the Rices and Linda and made his way to behind the stage. The marble bath was now empty and he noticed a small door at the back of the dais. He hesitated, and then went through it. Claudia was standing, patting herself dry with a towel. It was a very small office, and Claudia's clothes were scattered around in her usual untidy style. She was wearing the flesh-coloured swimsuit and it clung to her like a second skin.

She looked at him wearily. 'What now?'

He walked over to her and put his hands on her shoulders. 'I'm sorry,' he said, 'no more questions.'

37

She threw him her wide-eyed look, 'Promise?'

'I promise.'

She smiled then, and snaked her arms around his neck. 'All right then, you're forgiven.'

He bent down and kissed her warm soft lips. Her body was still wet and he put his hands in the top of her swimsuit and slowly peeled it off. 'Not here, you idiot,' she whispered, 'someone might come in. Anyway, you'll be missed.'

He let go of her, and went and turned the key in the door. She was giggling softly. 'Oh, David, you're really nutty!'

He cupped her breasts in his hands and bent to kiss them. She moaned, 'Go on then, you son of a bitch. Do whatever you want, I don't give a damn!'

CHAPTER SIX

The gathering at Monica's and Jack's was in full swing when Linda and David arrived. There were about ten people there, a mixed crowd, for Monica liked 'group variety' as she put it. Monica herself was a largish woman heading rapidly towards forty, and desperately trying to pull back the other way. She had a lot of very bright red hair, which was inclined to be frizzy, and her face, although heavily laden with Elizabeth Arden, was somewhat outdoorsy and even a little horsy. She used a heavy overpowering musky perfume, which enveloped you like her personality. She was given to talking in a shrieky sort of voice, and her conversation was always well peppered with 'dahling' and 'sweetie' and 'oh my God!'

Jack, in contrast, was rather reserved. He was a little older than David, but they had been close friends for a number of years. He smoked a pipe, and had a twirly grey moustache. He always wore suede jerkins, or some sort of similar sporty attire. One could imagine him with an enormous mansion tucked away in some rural part of England, walking some type of large dog through his spacious grounds. He owned a chain of garages, and in his younger days had fancied himself as a racing driver. Even now he would often take a test spin on the track to keep his hand in.

Monica grabbed hold of Linda when she arrived, and proudly, with her arm around her, she marched her into the living-room, where everyone was, and announced damatically, 'And this is our famous ban the bomber!'

Linda was terribly embarrassed, Monica made her sound like some new type of aeroplane! She knew most of the people there, and they all made some sign of greeting. There was one couple she hadn't met before, a thickset, very dark man, and a silver-blonde haughty-looking girl. Monica, as soon as she had finished with her dramatic announcement, introduced her.

'I'd like you to meet Jay and Lori Grossman, friends of mine from America. Jay's here to direct the new Conrad Lee picture.'

'Oh really,' said Linda, 'how interesting. I met a girl earlier this evening who's going to be in it.'

Jay raised a quizzical eyebrow. 'That is interesting,' he spoke with a short sharp New York accent, 'we haven't cast at all yet apart from the male star.'

'Oh well,' Linda smiled, 'I expect she's suffering from delusions.'

'What's her name anyway?' Jay asked.

Linda frowned. 'I can't really remember. My husband would know, she just did a commercial for his company.'

Just then Monica arrived with David, and made the introductions again. He had been in a very good mood since leaving the other party, and he put his arm around Linda and started to chat easily to the Grossmans.

'Darling,' Linda interrupted him, 'what was the name of that little girl who was doing the Beauty Maid thing?'

'What?' asked David, feeling at once guilty. 'Why do you want to know?'

Linda looked at him strangely, or anyway he thought she looked at him strangely. 'Do I have to have a reason?' she asked.

David felt slight tension build in the short silence that followed, and then at once he laughed weakly and said, 'Of course not. It's Claudia Parker, why?'

Jay shook his head. 'Never heard of her.'

'What is this?' questioned David.

'Well,' said Linda, 'you remember she said she was going to be in the new Conrad Lee picture. Well Jay's directing it, I thought he would know about her. Anyway apparently she isn't in it or going to be.'

'She didn't say she was going to be in it at all,' said David coldly, 'she said she had been to see Conrad Lee and he liked her, that's all.'

'Oh,' Jay laughed, 'that accounts for the confusion. Conrad is always seeing these poor little chicks and stringing them along. Actually, confidentially, the girl is already cast. An unknown Italian kid of sixteen. It builds up the publicity for a film though if we put on a big search for the right girl, and Conrad enjoys seeing the chicks so everyone is happy.'

David scowled at him. 'Everyone is happy except the poor little girls whose hopes he builds up.'

Jay shrugged, 'That's show biz, most of them know the score, and the ones that don't soon learn.' He turned to his wife who so far hadn't opened her mouth. 'Isn't that so, honey?'

Lori Grossman nodded. Her face never seemed to register any expression. It was like a beautiful, but quite blank, painted doll.

'That's how Lori and I met,' Jay continued, 'she was an actress, came for a part, and instead got me. She's my third wife, the other two were actresses as well. I probably met them the same way, don't even remember now.'

At last Lori spoke. Her voice was a thick Southern drawl. 'I sure would like another drink, honey.'

'Certainly baby,' Jay stood up. 'How about you, Mrs. Cooper?'

'Please call me Linda. I'd love a gin and tonic.'

Jay went off to fetch the drinks, and Monica arrived back and claimed Linda, dragging her over to some other people to show them the famous newspaper cutting.

Lori crossed long shapely legs.

David said, 'What part of America are you from?'

'I come from Georgia, honey,' she blinked lazily at him, 'but I've lived in Hollywood for the last five years.'

David studied her. She was older than Claudia, about twenty-seven he reckoned. She looked like one of those thin models out of *Vogue* magazine, everything carefully perfect. He found himself attracted to her. The very perfection made him wonder what she was like in bed. He wondered if that beautiful chignon silver-blonde hair stayed in place, one somehow couldn't imagine her with it out of place. 'How long are you here for?' he asked.

'Several months, I guess,' she drawled. She apparently had no conversation except to answer questions.

There was a silence until David said, 'You and your husband must come over to our house for dinner one night.'

'That would be fun.' She smiled at him, displaying two rows of even, white, obviously capped teeth.

Jay returned with the drinks. 'Where's that lovely wife of yours?' he asked David.

'Honey, there's no ice in this drink,' said Lori petulantly.

'Oh, screw the ice,' said Jay, 'this is England, baby, they don't go so big on the ice bit.' He turned to David, 'Listen, we have to meet some friends soon at the Candy Club, how about you and Linda coming along with us?'

'This is our second party tonight, and I don't know how tired Linda is, but it sounds like a good idea. I'll ask her.'

'Hell, you must come,' said Jay. 'Lori does the craziest cha cha cha you've ever seen. I'll go and ask Linda myself.' He went off.

Lori said, 'Gee honey, what do you do without ice!'

David laughed. 'We usually have ice, we're not that uncivilized. I suppose they've run out.'

She screwed up her nose. 'I like ice,' she stated, and then stared blankly off into space.

David looked at his watch, it was past twelve. Claudia would be safely at home in bed. After the incident in the office she had promised that she was going straight home, 'You've left me fit for nothing else!' she had joked. He wondered if he could telephone her, but then decided it was too late; he didn't want to wake her, and anyway there was nowhere really private that he could 'phone from. The Candy Club sounded like a good idea, and Lori Grossman's cha cha even better.

Jay returned with Linda, smiling broadly. 'I never get no for an answer,' he said with a wink, 'we're all set. Shall we make a move?'

Monica was quite frosty when she found David and Linda departing with the Grossmans. 'Well honestly, darlings,' she said, 'you've only been here two seconds!'

However they left, and piled into David's Jaguar.

Lori was wrapped in a full length black diamond mink

41

coat, and it reminded David that he had promised Claudia a jacket. He would get it the next day, she had been so sweet earlier. Or was sweet the right word?

Linda and Jay hit it off very well. They chatted away about the difference between England and America, and schools, and where it was best to bring up children, it seemed that Jay had three children, all from his previous marriages. Eventually Jay said to David, 'Hey, your wife is a doll! She's beautiful *and* intelligent, quite a combination.'

Linda was beginning to feel much bettter, her headache had gone, and she had had just enough drink to take away any tiredness and make her feel quite gay. She had pushed Paul away to the back of her mind, and was enjoying talking to Jay.

They arrived at the night-club. Jay made a grand entrance, as most Americans do, and asked to be taken to Mr. Lee's table.

The great Conrad Lee was a tall, voluble, half French, half White Russian man in his late fifties. He was totally bald, very suntanned, with piercing eyes which seemed to glare right through you, even in the dimness of the night-club.

He was at a table with six other people, and he leaped up and embraced Lori, and when Linda was introduced he kissed her hand. He smelled strongly of garlic.

The waiters busied themselves trying to squeeze more chairs around the already crowded table, and Jay attempted a few introductions, but it was more or less hopeless, as the noise of the band was so loud that you couldn't hear yourself speak anyway.

David stared in amazement and fury at Claudia. She sat beside Conrad, her hair tousled, one strap of her dress falling off her shoulder, much cleavage. She was very drunk. When Conrad sat down his hand caressed her shoulder, pushing the other strap of her dress down. There was another girl on the other side of Conrad, a plump brunette. He had his arm around her too, pinching chunks of her fleshy back between his fingers.

'Got two lovely girls here,' Conrad said to Jay, and then with a wink, 'maybe we can use them in the picture.'

Jay raised an eyebrow at Linda. 'See what I mean,' he said with a smile.

'That's the girl I was talking about,' Linda whispered.

'Sure,' said Jay, 'she's got as much chance of getting in the picture as fly!'

Claudia noticed David then, she was too drunk to be surprised or shocked. She just waved gaily, and said, 'What a small world!'

David remembered her saying those exact words to him the first time they had met. He scowled at her.

Conrad took Lori off to dance, then Jay claimed Linda, and they went off to dance too.

David sat down in the now empty chair beside Claudia. 'You lousy little bitch!' he said in a low voice. 'Going straight home to bed, well I suppose you'll be doing that eventually.'

She looked surprised. 'Baby, what's the matter? I did go home, and then Conrad called and said he would like to see me again, so he could come to some decision about the part. Well, I mean I have to think about my career, don't I?'

'You're drunk,' he said with disgust, 'you're acting like a whore. Do you honestly believe all this shit Conrad is telling you about putting you in his stinking film? I credited you with more brains than that.'

She looked at him coldly. 'Oh piss off, David, you make me sick. You're just jealous, that's all. The only time you act sweet is when you've got a hard on!'

He wanted to slap her. She sat there, glaring at him, and for one lucid moment he saw not his beautiful Claudia, but a hard calculating face over a well developed, highly exhibited body.

'Your tits are hanging out!' he said.

'So?' she replied. 'Why not? Are you the only one that's supposed to see them?'

The plump brunette the other side of David suddenly tugged his arm. 'Are you a film producer too?' she asked. Her eyes were large and round and somewhat bloodshot.

'No,' he said curtly.

Conrad and Lori returned to the table, and David stood up. Lori was very tall. She stood there remote and cool. David could see that Claudia was watching her jealously. He took hold of Lori's arms quickly. 'What about another dance?' he said. 'I want to see this wild cha cha of yours.'

Claudia shot him a dirty look, and then focused her charm on Conrad again.

'That would be fun, honey,' drawled Lori, and they headed for the dance floor.

She danced beautifully. 'I used to be a showgirl in Vegas,' she confided.

The evening dragged on. Claudia got drunker and drunker, and she and Conrad closer and closer. The plump brunette was obviously forgotten. Linda and Jay chatted on. Lori sat silently, only speaking when someone spoke to her. David lounged morosely watching Claudia and Conrad, and occasionally attempting to flirt with Lori in case Claudia should be watching him.

At two in the morning Linda eventually said to him, with a yawn, 'I think we had better be going, I'm absolutely tired out.'

No one else in the party seemed interested in leaving, so they said goodbye, and David tried to press some money on Jay, as their part of the bill, but Jay refused to accept it. Claudia said goodbye with a drunken smile, and then turned back to concentrate on Conrad, who by this time was as drunk as she was.

Jay insisted on coming with them to the car, and they exchanged 'phone numbers and promised to all get together again soon.

At last they were alone. Linda leaned back in the car and closed her eyes. David said, not really meaning it, but wanting to take his bad temper out on someone, 'You and that phoney director were getting very friendly.'

She opened her eyes. 'No more friendly than you and that tatty soap model.'

He shot her a dark look. 'I didn't even talk to her, I don't know what you mean.'

'Oh, David, really,' she sighed, 'you didn't even talk to anyone you were so annoyed she was with Conrad Lee. Any fool could see that.' She paused, then added curiously, 'Have you ever taken her out?'

He stared furiously at the road ahead. 'What a ridiculous question.'

'I just wondered, I mean you seemed so sort of interested in her. Even at the first party you kept on getting in little huddles with her.'

'She works for us, Linda, I was trying to see that the display went off smoothly, that's all.'

They lapsed into silence. He switched the car radio on.

'Darling,' Linda said quickly, tentatively, 'what's wrong?'

'What do you mean what's wrong?'

'I mean what's wrong with us? What's happening to us? Why are we so far apart all of a sudden?'

He turned off the radio. 'I didn't know we were so far apart.'

She looked out of the car window, they were driving through the park, and the trees looked dark and ominous as they sped past them. 'It's funny, David, this must have been starting to happen to us for years, and yet neither of us realized it, neither of us tried to stop it. We're almost like strangers now, two strangers, and the only thing we have in common are our children.'

'I think you're overtired, you're talking a lot of nonsense.'

'A lot of nonsense,' she repeated, 'is that what you really think?' Tears started to roll silently down her cheeks. 'When did you last make love to me? When did you last really want to?'

'Oh, so that's what this is about.'

She fought to keep the tears under control. 'No, that's not what all this is about, but I suppose it's a part of it.'

He pulled the car into the side of the road and stopped, and then turned to face her. What could he say? That he didn't find her very exciting any more? That Claudia was a better lay? She was right, really, they were far apart.

'Do you remember our honeymoon?' she questioned.

Yes, he remembered their honeymoon. Spain, hot and sticky and long pleasurable nights with Linda; an innocent young Linda, who awoke all sorts of desires and ambitions in him. 'Yes, I remember our honeymoon,' he said quietly.

'Why can't things be like they were then?' She looked at him plaintively.

'Linda, we're both ten years older. Things don't stand still, you know.'

'Yes, I know.' She thought – Paul makes me feel ten years younger. He makes me feel attractive and desirable. He makes me feel wanted.

David said, 'We'd better be getting home. I want to get to the office early in the morning.'

'Yes, all right.' She thought – Why don't you take me in

45

your arms? Why don't you throw me down on the back seat and make love to me here?

They drove home in an uneasy silence, both realizing that there was more unsaid than said.

The house seemed cold and dark. Linda went in to look at the children. Jane slept curled up in a ball, her thumb stuck firmly in her mouth. Stephen had kicked all his covers off, and had nearly fallen out of bed. She covered him, and kissed him lightly on the forehead. They were so innocent, her two precious children. So young and pure.

David was taking a shower. Linda undressed and settled into bed. She wondered if because of what she had said, he would want to make love tonight.

He didn't. He returned from the bathroom, got into bed, switched the light off, muttered, 'Goodnight', and appeared to go straight off to sleep.

She lay there angry and frustrated. I tried, she thought, I really tried to talk to him. But he doesn't seem to care what's happening to us, he doesn't seem to *mind*.

The morning dawned bleak and raining.

David was up at seven. He shaved, showered, and dressed without disturbing Linda, and was out of the house by eight.

She awoke shortly after. Jane was standing beside the bed. 'Mummy, can I come in for a cuddle, please?' she requested.

'Yes, of course, darling.'

'I hate Stevie,' Jane confided, 'he's a nasty rough boy. I wish boys were girls!'

'Yes, that's a very good idea,' replied Linda, smilingly.

The morning passed in a flurry of domesticity. The children started at school the following day, and there was a lot to be done. School uniforms to be assembled, books to be found, everything clean.

Linda had no time to think, and in the afternoon she had promised to take them to the news theatre to see the cartoons.

There was no message from Paul. She was both hurt and yet relieved.

When they returned from the cinema she 'phoned David. He wasn't in the office; she left a message for him to call her as soon as he returned.

Jay Grossman had 'phoned and left a number, she rang him back. 'We were wondering if you and David would
46

care to join us for dinner tomorrow night?' he said. 'Lori just can't wait to go to the Savoy Grill, she's heard Princess Margaret goes there, and figures we're bound to be at the next table!'

Linda laughed, 'I'll have to check with David, can you possibly call us back later?'

David didn't phone until past seven. 'I'll be late,' he said.

'How late?'

'How the hell do I know, probably around twelve.'

'Where do you have to go?'

His voice was angry. 'What is this, a cross examination?'

She replied coldly, 'No, it's not a cross examination, but I think I'm entitled to know why you're going to be late.'

There was a silence, then, 'I'm sorry, of course you're entitled to know. I'm tired, I suppose. Actually I've got a late discussion with Phillip.'

'Well, why don't you bring him back here and I'll give you both some dinner.'

'No, it's all right, we'll get a sandwich next door and get on with things.'

'I'll see you later then.'

'Yes, don't wait up.' He hesitated, then asked, 'How are the children?'

'They're fine. In a state of excitement about school tomorrow.'

'Give them a kiss for me. 'Bye.'

''Bye.' She hung up and yawned. It's an early night for me, she thought, then she remembered that Jay would be phoning back about dinner the following evening. Quickly she picked up the 'phone, and dialled David's private number at the office. It rang and rang, but there was no reply.

'Oh bother,' she muttered. She hung up and went and looked in the phone book for Phillip's number, David was probably in *his* office. She couldn't find Phillip's office number, but his home number was there, so she dialled that. His wife Mary answered.

'I'm sorry to bother you,' said Linda, 'but can you give me Phillip's private number at the office?'

'Yes, of course,' said Mary, sounding slightly surprised, 'but I'm expecting him home any minute, so I shouldn't think there would be any reply.'

47

Now it was Linda's turn to sound surprised. 'But isn't he working late with David?'

'No, he's definitely on his way home, his mother is here for dinner, he'll be here any minute now.'

'Oh,' said Linda quietly, 'I must have made a mistake.'

'Hang on a sec,' said Mary, 'I think I hear him at the door now.'

Linda was left hanging numbly on to the receiver. She felt stunned. So David was lying. Why was he lying? How long had he been lying? And why was it only now, when she herself had been unfaithful, that she had to find out? It was obviously another woman. She felt sick.

Phillip's slightly harsh voice boomed down the 'phone. 'Hello Linda. What's your problem?'

She forced her voice to be light. 'Oh, no problem, Phillip, I'm just trying to track David down. I thought he said he was working with you, but I must have got it wrong.'

Phillip sounded embarrassed, 'Well actually I can't help you. David left the office early today.' He added as an after-thought, 'he's probably out with Mr. Smythson or someone from up north, we seem to have a whole group of people down this week.'

'Thank you, Phillip,' said Linda, she wanted to say – you don't have to try and make excuses for him, instead she said, 'I'm sure you're right, goodbye.'

So this was it. This was the answer to all her questions. It all tied in, late nights home, week-ends away on business, no real physical interest in her. This must have been subconsciously why she found herself in bed with Paul. They say there is a certain point in every marriage where a woman is at the crossroads as to whether to go to bed with someone else or not and, depending on the state of her marriage at the time, she makes her decision.

It's true, thought Linda, if things had been all right with David and me, then I would never have looked twice at that boy. She started to cry. It all seemed so wrong, and to add insult to injury Paul hadn't even rung her.

She threw herself down on the sofa, and gave way to her tears. 'I hate men,' she sobbed, 'selfish, lousy, horrible bastards ...'

CHAPTER SEVEN

David awoke on Tuesday morning early, with one thought uppermost in his mind, and that was to get out of the house, reach a telephone, and 'phone Claudia.

It was seven o'clock and Linda lay sleeping quietly, so quietly in fact that for a moment he contemplated using the phone in the house, but realizing the probable folly of this decided against it.

He shaved, showered, dressed hurriedly, and left. He drove as far as Baker Street before stopping to use the 'phone. It rang dully in Claudia's flat, but no one answered it. He re-dialled, but still no reply. He let it ring for a long time but to no avail. At last he reached the obvious conclusion that she was either out, or too deeply asleep to be disturbed.

He jumped back into his car, and with a sudden flash of decision drove to where she lived.

This time it was the doorbell he rang to no avail.

'Little bitch!' he muttered to himself, 'dirty little bitch!'

He hung around outside for a while, but eventually realizing the futility of this, he drove sourly to his office.

Every half hour he rang her number, getting more and more angry each time it wasn't answered. Until at last, at eleven, it was finally picked up by Claudia's daily.

'Is Miss Parker there please?'

The daily's voice was full of Cockney richness. 'I fink she's asleep. 'Old on a tick, I'll go an' 'ave a look.' She returned after a short pause. 'She ain't in,' she stated. 'Any message?'

He said, 'You don't happen to know what time she went out?'

'Can't say that I do. Don't fink she's bin in since yesterday, 'cos 'er bed ain't been slept in.'

'Thank you,' said David, 'there's no message.'

He imagined her with Conrad. Her smooth, beautiful body crushed to his, going through the motions of love

49

which she practised so expertly. He could almost hear her small exquisite cries of excitement, her little moans, and the way she mutttered crude words in a low throaty voice. He swore.

After that he rang her flat every hour, hanging up when the daily answered. He was furious with himself for being in such a state about her. He had always prided himself on never getting too deeply involved emotionally, always being able to shut other people out of his life when he had had enough of them. But this time it was different. Whatever she did, he couldn't seem to get Claudia out of his mind.

At four o'clock she finally picked up her 'phone. The record player was very loud in the background, and she sounded in good spirits. He listened to her voice saying 'Hello,' then a pause, then – 'Hello, is anyone there?' Then another longer pause, and then – 'Oh, screw you whoever it is!' And the 'phone was slammed down.

He left the office at once, and drove straight over to where she lived. He didn't want to row with her on the 'phone, he wanted to see her, hear the excuses, watch her lie.

She answered her front door and looked surprised and a little guilty to see him. She was wearing very tight white slacks, and a large black polo-necked sweater. Her face was devoid of any make-up, and although she looked a little tired, her brilliant green eyes shone with an alert, triumphant expression.

'Well, surprise, surprise!' she said. 'Come on in.'

He followed her into the flat. A very loud Sinatra singing 'Come Fly With Me', was turned up full volume. A half bottle of Scotch, and a giant pink fluffy toy poodle stood on the table.

'Want a drink?' asked Claudia.

'It's four o'clock in the afternoon,' he said coldly.

'Square . . .' she muttered, like a naughty child caught doing something wrong.

She poured herself a stiff Scotch, lit a cigarette, and flopped down on the floor. 'Well, David, what is there to say?'

'There's plenty to say,' he paced the room angrily, and added menacingly, 'plenty.'

She giggled, 'Oh stop it with the wronged husband bit. I *told* you I wasn't tied to anyone. I warned you that no man tells me what to do.'

50

He shook his head at her, 'I don't understand you, you act like some cheap little whore.'

She rolled over on her stomach, taking a long drag of her cigarette and, blowing the smoke towards him, said calmly, 'I'm in a very good mood today, nothing can spoil it, not even you.' She rolled on to her back and stretched, the taut outline of her breasts appearing through her sweater. He felt the familiar hot desire creep up on him.

'Conrad Lee is a very important man, and he's going to do a lot for me.'

'Oh yes, he'll do a lot for you,' said David bitterly, 'he'll do a lot for you in bed.'

'I'm testing this week for his new film, how about that?'

'Balls!'

'Oh, you're just jealous, that's all. You see, he's going to make a star out of me. You wait, you'll see.'

'You're making a fool out of yourself, the *director* of the film said that this is Conrad's hobby, stringing along little girls like you.'

'I'm not a little girl. I'm a big girl. I'm not a fool, I do know the score.'

'How was he in the sack?'

Her eyes met his. They were big and green and bright. 'He wasn't anything like you.' She stood up, and wrapped her arms around him. 'No one's like you,' she whispered, 'no one's ever been like you.' The fight was over.

It was slow, and warm, and tender. Afterwards they lay on the floor where he had taken her, locked in each other's arms.

She kissed him softly. 'You must understand,' she whispered, 'it doesn't mean I don't love you. When I sleep with him it's nothing. He's a pig, an old pig. But baby, I want to be in his film, I want to be in it so much. I'm going to be in it, I promise you that.'

He flicked his hands over her soft breasts. 'You're so beautiful, when I'm with you I don't care what you've been doing. All right then, get in his lousy movie if you must. But don't sleep with him or anyone else again, or I'll beat hell out of you!'

She pressed closer to him. 'I wish you would beat me, that would be good.'

It's impossible, he thought, impossible that it could happen again so soon, and be that much better. She's like a

51

tigress. They could cage her naked in the zoo for all to see, for only seeing is believing: and they should pin a notice to her cage – 'Do not feed, only eats men.'

Out of the blue Claudia said, 'Your wife's very attractive, isn't she?'

'She used to be. I suppose she still is really.'

'How old is she?' asked Claudia, a typical woman's question.

David wasn't interested in discussing Linda. 'Oh thirty something, I don't know.'

'I wonder what I'll look like when I'm thirty.'

He was saved from answering this by the telephone ringing. Claudia reluctantly lifted her receiver.

'Oh, hello,' she said softly. She glanced quickly over at David. He immediately wondered who it was. 'I'd like that,' she was saying, 'about what time?' She balanced the receiver under her chin, and fumbled for a cigarette from the table. 'All right then, see you tomorrow. Look forward to it.' She hung up. 'I'm starving!' she exclaimed. 'I feel like going out for a fabulous exciting dinner.'

'Who was that?' he asked, trying to keep his voice casual.

'Who was what?' she asked, knowing perfectly well what he meant.

'On the 'phone.'

'Oh, that!' she hesitated for just a second too long before saying. 'It was my agent. He wanted me to have dinner with him and his wife tomorrow night.'

'Friendly of him, just like that he starts asking you to dinner.'

'Yes, just like that,' she said patiently. 'As a matter of fact I called him earlier and told him I wanted to see him about this Conrad thing. I'm going to bathe, can we go out later? Or have you got to rush home?'

He thought she was lying, but what was the point in arguing. 'Do you want me to be free?'

'Silly! Of course I want you to be free, otherwise I wouldn't have asked you.'

'I'll 'phone home, where do you want to go, I'll book a table.'

'Oh, let's go somewhere swinging for a change. We always have to hide out in some old dive. What does it matter if we're seen. After all I am Miss Beauty Maid, so I'm business really! Let's go to Carlo's.'

Carlo's was a fairly new, very expensive, very fashionable Italian restaurant. It was *the* place to go, *the* place to be seen at. He knew that he was taking a ridiculous risk going there with Claudia. He was sure that he would see people he knew there. However, on the other hand, he wanted to be seen with Claudia, he wanted people to know that this was his. Then also, Claudia wanted to go there, and now she had him by the short hairs, and they both knew it. He had come running back after what she had done, and now it was she who was able to call the tune.

'O.K., you go and make yourself pretty, and I'll book a table for eight o'clock.'

She kissed him lightly. 'Divine, darling.'

He gave her a playful tap on the bottom. 'Go put some clothes on, or we'll never get out!'

Giggling, she retired to the bathroom.

David read the evening papers, booked a table at the restaurant. He felt guilty about phoning Linda, but eventually he did, and then snapped at her when she asked what he had to do. He produced some suitable lies, felt badly about the whole thing, enquired after the children in a fit of conscience, and then hung up.

Claudia reappeared after a time, transformed. Her glossy ash-blonde hair was piled on the top of her head in studied confusion, her make-up was smooth and perfect. She wore a plain black dress, and rows and rows of jet beads. She looked stunning.

David told her so, and she smiled and preened and showed off her dress to him, flirting around the room, like some beautiful exotic bird. 'Isn't it *exciting* going out somewhere *decent* together!' she exclaimed. 'I do wish we could do it more often.'

In the car on the way to the restaurant he had second thoughts. It was a stupid thing to do. Linda was bound to find out, and then what? Especially as she seemed to be so sensitive about their marriage lately. He glanced quickly over at Claudia, she was fiddling with the radio trying to find some music on it.

'Why don't we drive out somewhere nice in the country instead?'

She looked over to him, her eyes frosty. 'I knew you'd get cold feet, *you* go to the country, drop me at a cab rank, I'm sick of hiding all over the place.'

'All right, we'll go to Carlo's.' To hell with it, Linda probably wouldn't find out, they said that wives were always the last to know.

The restaurant was very crowded. The head waiter said their table would be a few minutes, so they sat in the bar. Claudia greeted several people. David was relieved to see no one he knew.

A girl came up to them, dragging a weedy-looking young chap behind her. She was very thin and sun-tanned, and quite pretty. 'Darling!' she said to Claudia, 'you look fabulous! Where *have* you been, haven't seen you for ages!' She dragged the young man alongside her. '*You* remember Jeremy.' Jeremy blushed and stuttered 'Hello'. 'Well darling, we're engaged! Can you imagine!' she giggled and gave Jeremy a playful poke in the ribs. He looked acutely embarrassed.

'Shirley!' exclaimed Claudia. 'How marvellous!' She turned to David, 'Shirl darling, this is David Cooper, a very old friend of mine.'

Shirley extended a small suntanned hand, and David shook it briefly.

Claudia continued, 'And David, I'd like you to meet Shirley's fiancé, the Hon. Jeremy Francis.'

Jeremy edged forward. 'Jolly glad to meet you, old boy.' He had sandy-coloured skin, liberally dotted with angry red spots.

'Sit down and have a drink,' said Claudia, 'we must celebrate!'

They found extra chairs and sat down. The girls immediately went into a huddle about the dresses they were wearing. The Hon. Jeremy sat uncomfortably on the edge of his chair. He was extremely tall, and his knees bumped David's under the table.

'We're going to have an *enormous* wedding,' Shirley was now saying, 'it will be simply marvellous. Jeremy's parents know absolutely everyone!' She flashed a large emerald and diamond ring at Claudia. 'Look!' she said dramatically. 'Asprey's!'

Claudia said, 'It's divine, I love it. I'm so happy for you both.

'And now what about *you?*' questioned Shirley, shooting a coy, meaningful look at David.

Claudia laughed. 'You know how *I* feel about marriage.

54

It's not for me, Shirl baby. I dig the single bit. Anyway *you* met Jeremy first!'

Jeremy blushed, and looked suitably flattered.

David stood up. 'I think our table's ready.'

'Oh, did you *book*?' said Shirley wistfully. 'We forgot, and now we've got to wait simply ages for a table, and I'm *starving*.' She hesitated for a second or two, and then continued, 'I say, why don't we all have dinner together. I haven't seen you for *such* ages Claudia, and it would be such fun!'

'We have a table for two,' said David grimly.

'Oh, well, we don't mind being a bit cramped, do we, Jeremy?'

Jeremy nodded blankly.

'What do you say?' Shirley turned to Claudia.

Claudia looked hopelessly at David. 'Fine, we'd love it.'

They followed the waiter to their table, Shirley waving and smiling to several people on the way. 'I think this is a simply marvellous place,' she said to Claudia as they reached their table. 'I'm sure if one just sat here for a week one would see absolutely everyone one ever knew pass by, sort of like London Airport!' She giggled loudly.

David sat through the dinner in sullen silence, and Jeremy didn't have much to say at any time, so it was Shirley who did all the talking, with Claudia occasionally joining in. Shirley was an avid reader of *Queen* magazine, especially the society pages, and her main topics of conversation were who had been seen with whom, and what good parties were going on. Jeremy apparently, was asked to most of them, and Shirley went into minute details about the most boring items. For example, Lady Clarissa Colt wearing the same dress to two different parties, and the Hon. Amanda Lawrence having a coming-out party where they ran out of champagne. 'It was too awful,' wailed Shirley, 'one just *never* should run short of champers! Too embarrassing!'

Eventually, when they had reached dessert, Jeremy took her off to the small dance floor, and they clung limply together to a Bossa Nova beat.

'Lets get out of here,' said David, 'I've heard just as much as I can take from that stupid, snotty little cow.'

'I'm sorry, baby,' replied Claudia soothingly, 'she is a bit much.'

'A bit much! That's an understatement if ever I heard one. Who is she anyway?'

A smile played softly around Claudia's mouth. 'When I first came to London I worked in a club, Miss Fancy Pants worked there too.'

'What were you doing in a club?' asked David surprised.

'Well darling, I had to earn some money, it doesn't grow on trees you know, and this actor I arrived with never seemed to work, so I took a job in this club.'

'Doing what?'

'The dance of the seven veils!' Claudia replied laughingly.

'What! You must be joking.'

Claudia's smile faded slightly. 'I'm not joking. Look I had no talent for doing anything else, it was either that, or being hostess and getting pawed about by a lot of dirty old men, and I would sooner take my clothes off any day. They could look, but they couldn't touch.'

'I don't know anything about you really, do I?'

Claudia's large eyes turned suddenly remote. 'You've never bothered to listen, like all men, your prime concern is to get me in the sack as fast as possible.'

There was a short silence, then Claudia gave a quick brittle laugh. 'I'm sorry, my past is a big drag anyway, why should you want to hear about it.'

David was about to reply when Shirley and Jeremy returned.

'Jeremy's made the most divine suggestion,' said Shirley. 'There is a simply dinky little night-club opened down at Windsor, and he says why don't we all pop down there.'

David looked at her sourly. 'At the Castle, naturally.'

For a moment Shirley's pale blue eyes glinted angrily, then she grimaced and laughed quickly, replying, '*No* sweetie, *not* at the Castle.'

'Count us out then,' said David.

'I say old chap, are you sure?' stammered Jeremy.

Claudia broke hurriedly into the conversation. 'David's a bit tired, you two run along, and if we change our minds we'll join you later.'

'All right then,' said Shirley, 'but *do* try and make it.' She grabbed Jeremy by the arm, 'Come along sweetie, we'll leave these two lovebirds on their own.'

She shot a dark glance at David, waved gaily at Claudia, and towing Jeremy along behind her, they made their exit.

Claudia started to laugh.

'I don't happen to think it's so funny,' said David grimly. 'I suppose I'm stuck with the bill as well. Many thanks for the delightful evening.'

Claudia's laughter increased. 'Oh, I'm sorry. But honestly it *is* funny. If you had known Shirley a few years ago, well I mean, you just wouldn't believe it. She was anybody's and everybody's!'

His tone was cold; 'And you?'

Abruptly Claudia stopped laughing. She stared at him for a few seconds, and then said slowly and deliberately, 'I think we have just about reached the end of our relationship, if you could ever call it that.' Before he had a chance to reply, she got up from the table, and threading her way through the restaurant she vanished out of sight. Quickly he called for his bill.

'It's David Cooper, isn't it?' the voice was loud and American.

David looked startled. There stood Jay Grossman. 'Well hello,' he said uneasily.

'Where is your lovely wife?' Jay stared pointedly at the obviously recently occupied place across the table.

David wondered if he had seen Claudia leave, then decided he hadn't, otherwise, as he was more or less only a casual acquaintance he would never have made such an obvious remark. 'Oh, she's at home,' said David, then indicating the rest of the table he continued, 'I had a business meeting, they all had to rush-off.'

At that moment the waiter presented the bill, and leaving a wad of notes David got up quickly.

'You must come on over to say "hello" to Lori,' said Jay, 'she would be most upset if I told her I'd seen you and hadn't brought you over for a drink.'

'Only for a minute then,' said David reluctantly. 'Linda's expecting me.'

The Grossmans were sitting at a table right across the other side of the room, and he was pleased to note that they couldn't see his table from where they were. Jay had only spotted him by chance on his way back from the men's room. Lori looked as aloof and perfectly groomed as before. Every shining blonde strand of hair arranged carefully in place, her face a mask of smooth clear flawless make-up. She wore a pale brown chiffon dress, which dipped revealingly between her breasts.

'Nice to see you again,' said David unable to keep his eyes from straying down her neckline.

'Likewise,' she replied, in her faintly suggestive, empty American drawl.

'Come on – sit down, you must join us for a drink,' said Jay.

'Well,' he sought wildly for an excuse, couldn't find one, and anyway, what the hell – eyes fixed firmly on Lori's neckline he sat down.

'What will you have?' asked Jay.

'A scotch on the rocks.'

Jay summoned the waiter while Lori produced a small gold compact and proceeded to touch up an already perfect make-up.

'I spoke to Linda earlier,' Jay said, 'she mentioned she was going to talk to you about joining us for dinner tomorrow night.'

'Oh,' said David blankly – his mind was half on the fact that Claudia had walked out on him – what a bitch! and half on the fact that he had a strong fancy for Mrs. Cool, dumb Grossman. What a revelation to get her into bed and penetrate beneath the layers of make-up, eyelashes, and hair pieces. 'That would be a good idea, where do you want to go?'

'Well, Lori wants to see the Savoy Grill.'

'Yeah,' Lori put down her compact for one brief moment, 'I've heard it's a gas. You get to see Princess Margaret and that cute guy she's married to.'

'They don't exactly do a cabaret there,' said David smiling, 'but they have been known to go there.'

Jay said, 'Shall we meet at our hotel?'

They chatted a short while longer, and then David made his excuses and left. He tipped the attendant who brought his car round, and sat morosely in it. Screw Miss Hot Pants Parker. She was becoming too much. First of all she talked him into going to a restaurant he didn't even want to go to, then she lumbered him with her dreary friends, then she admitted to working in a strip joint, and got insulted when he commented on it, and then had the utter cheek to get up and walk out on him. On top of all this she had been to bed with that fat slob of a producer the previous evening. She was nothing but a little tramp, an easy lay. If he wasn't dead careful he might even catch something from her. She could get lost, he was going home.

He headed his car towards Hampstead. It was ten o'clock.

CHAPTER EIGHT

After a while Linda stopped crying. She went into the bathroom and washed her face, her eyes were red and swollen. She stared at her reflection in the mirror. She didn't know what to do, she knew she couldn't face the prospect of sitting around waiting for David to finally arrive home, fresh from the arms of some tart. She had no one to telephone. Since marrying, she had gradually lost touch with all her girl-friends – they had all drifted apart, got married and gone off to live in different parts of the country. She thought of 'phoning her mother, but to confide in her would be ridiculous. Her mother had never really approved of David, and would be only too pleased. She had warned Linda against marrying him. 'After all, he's a Jew,' she had said, as if that explained everything.

In desperation she 'phoned Monica, she had to talk to someone.

Monica was cool. 'Well dahling, absolutely charming the way you stayed five minutes and then dragged off my most important guests. I mean, really dahling – a bit off.'

Their conversation was brief, and when Linda hung up she thought – the hell with it, I'm not a child and she picked up the phone again and dialled Paul's number.

He answered the phone – 'Hello?'

She got cold feet and froze not saying anything, quickly she hung up the receiver. It rang again almost immediately. She said 'Hello'.

'Linda this is Paul, I know you just 'phoned me.'

59

She was taken aback.

'Look – I've been waiting for you to 'phone. Can I see you? Can you come over?'

'When?' she muttered weakly.

'Can you make it now?'

'Well, I don't know . . .'

'Please I must talk to you.'

'Well, all right then, I'll be there in half-an-hour.'

'Great,' he gave her the address.

She was surprised. Ego had told her that he wouldn't have forgotten her, but she hadn't expected him to be waiting to see her, expecting her to 'phone.

She got ready swiftly, before she changed her mind, and drove the five-minute distance to where he lived. It was an old house converted into flats squashed between a butcher's shop and a vet on the main High Street. She climbed five flights of stairs before reaching his flat – number 8, with a peeling yellow front door.

He answered her knock immediately.

'I don't really know what I'm doing here,' she blurted out. He took her by the hand and led her inside.

'You look lovely, I've been going mad waiting for you to 'phone.'

'Why didn't you 'phone me?'

'Look Linda – I dig your scene. I didn't want to put you in a bad position, it was up to you to make the next move.'

He made her feel very young, although she could give him at least ten years.

'I know nothing about you.'

'You're always saying that,' replied Paul. He was wearing paint-stained faded old blue jeans, and a white polo-neck sweater. He looked very attractive.

They were standing in a small dark room which Linda presumed was the lounge, dining room, study, etc. The walls were painted black and hung with lots of paintings, some framed, some unframed, mostly nudes with exotic thin faces, masses of hair and voluptuous bodies. The furniture in the room was a teak Danish dining-table – piled high with papers, and a battered old scarlet sofa. She sat on the sofa and he said she could have a beer or 90% proof Russian Vodka – brought direct from Moscow by a friend of his. She elected to have the Vodka. It was very strong, he

60

mixed it with water and it tasted vile, but she struggled to get it down. He put a Billie Holliday record on and sat beside her.

'Look, about the other night,' she said nervously, 'it should never have happened – I mean well – I'd had a row with my husband and I had too much to drink ...'

He took her hand. 'You don't have to make excuses, it happened and it was great, and if you're embarrassed about it, well you didn't have to see me again. I didn't call you for that reason.'

She took another gulp of vodka. 'I just wanted to explain!' she hesitated and then rushed on, 'I mean I didn't want to leave you with the wrong impression of me.'

'You left me with a beautiful impression, your perfume was all over my bed and the smell of your body, and the way you cried out when you came.' He reached over for her and she half-heartedly tried to pull away. But their mouths met and she was lost. He was young and trying to please and full of strength, and this time she was almost sober. His whole feeling seemed to be to try and please her, and in return she found herself twice as adept at thrilling him. They made love for two hours – starting on the sofa, the floor, and then the bedroom. Afterwards they lay and talked.

She felt so peaceful and protected by him. He listened quietly while she told him about David and his indifference towards her. She told him everything about herself, about the children, about her life. They smoked cigarettes and drank more vodka.

She found out about him too. He was an artist, he had left Art School a year before and was now working as assistant to the Art Editor of a glossy woman's magazine. The paintings on the wall and in the other room were all his. She found out they were of a girl-friend he had called Margarethe. It was a sad story, they had met at Art School and fallen madly in love. Margarethe was from Sweden, and had worked as an au pair girl for three years to earn enough money to study art. She was a lovely girl and after living together for six months they decided to get married. Paul's mother was dead and his father, a retired businessman lived in Cheltenham. So to the house in Cheltenham they went to have Margarethe meet father. She met father and three days later she married him. Paul was stunned, he couldn't

61

believe it. He had a terrible row with both of them, and hadn't seen or heard from them since.

'I couldn't accept it,' Paul said, 'I mean, I don't believe she could have loved him, I suppose she wanted his loot, I couldn't offer her any security.'

'How do you feel about her now?' questioned Linda.

'I don't know,' said Paul moodily. 'I think she's a cow. They just went off one afternoon and came back married.'

'Why do you still keep your paintings of her around?'

'I don't know,' he shrugged, 'just to remind me not to be such a berk again, I suppose. I can't make it with girls any more, y'know. Maybe once or twice, then I just don't want to know.'

She remembered whiney voiced, pretty little Melanie.

'I imagine I'm all right because I'm married?' said Linda.

'Yeah, I guess so, but listen darling, I really do dig you. I think you're great.'

They lay in silence for a while, both mulling over their individual problems.

'The thing that really gets me,' said Paul, 'is imagining Margarethe living in Cheltenham with my old man. She was such a swinger, really a cuke. She liked to ball more than anyone I ever knew. I just can't see her fancying him. He's a drag.'

'What was your mother like?' asked Linda.

'It's a long story,' said Paul.

Linda leaned over and kissed him lightly on the forehead. 'Tell me about it,' she said gently.

'You sound like a psychiatrist,' he laughed. 'Actually it's a lousy story, she killed herself when I was fifteen.'

There was silence. Linda was shocked. She wanted to ask why – but Paul had turned over on his side, and closed his eyes. 'It's a drag, Linda,' he muttered, 'I'll tell you about it some other time.'

After a while Linda looked at her watch and seeing that it was past eleven, she said, 'Look, I had better be leaving, David's going to be home at twelve.'

'Can't you stay the night?' Paul mumbled, his back still to her.

'Oh, honestly Paul, I would like to but I just can't not be there when he gets home – I mean he would be worried. He knows I never stay out – he'd probably call the police.'

'It's funny, isn't it,' Paul said. 'All these little birds that I bang I just can't get rid of.' He put on a high thin voice, 'Oh darling, let me stay the night – Mummy and Daddy never expect me before morning.' They both laughed.

'I tell you it's horrible, they just will not go. And you must know what it's like to screw someone and then not be able to stand them near you after. Y'know Linda, you're the first female since Margarethe I've asked to stay the night – and you say no.'

She dressed slowly and Paul lay lazily back in bed watching her.

'Y'know, you're very sexy, I'd dig seeing you in long black nylons and a black garter belt.'

'What would you do, take pictures?'

'No – I'd paint you – sort of lying on the sofa. Very sexy indeed. Can I?'

'I'll think about it,' she laughed, slightly embarrassed.

Eventually she was ready to go.

'When am I going to see you?' he asked.

'Well, I don't know.'

'Tomorrow?'

'I don't know Paul, it's very difficult for me to make plans.'

'You can't just leave without telling me when.'

'I'll 'phone you in the morning.'

He gave her his 'phone number at work, kissed her long and hard, and she set off on her journey home. It was eleven thirty.

CHAPTER NINE

Claudia left the restaurant angrily. She hailed a taxi and directed it to Conrad Lee's hotel. She was fed up with David Cooper. Stupid bastard – who did he think he was! At first their affaire had been fun. She dug having affaires with married men, they were a race apart, and always a challenge. Also, she had misguidedly thought he might be able to help

63

her career. Nothing he had done, absolutely nothing. Being Miss Beauty Maid appeared to lead to a dead end. He hadn't even given her a decent present, just a lot of unkept promises. So where was the famous mink jacket she was supposed to get? She didn't want money from him, how dare he offer her money like some cheap whore, but presents were a different matter.

'Cheapskate,' she muttered under her breath. 'Why he even complained about paying the bill in the restaurant.'

The taxi pulled up at the hotel and a doorman leaped forward to escort her in. She strolled coolly over to reception.

'I'd like to speak to Mr. Conrad Lee.'

They put her through on the house 'phone. After a while the operator said there was no reply.

'Would you try the 'phone in the bedroom please,' said Claudia.

The 'phone rang several times, then a voice answered thickly – 'Yeah?'

'Conrad, this is Claudia Parker.'

'Who?'

'Claudia Parker,' she repeated patiently. 'Listen darling, you can't have forgotten last night already?'

There was a short pause, then – 'Oh yeah, of course, how are you baby? What can I do for you?'

'Well, your secretary called me earlier about seeing you tomorrow night – I was out with this dreary guy, and I suddenly thought the hell with it, what about tonight.'

He laughed, coughed unattractively and said, 'Listen baby, I'm all tied up tonight.'

'Oh,' she sounded disappointed. 'Look, I'm cool,' she continued, 'I never find three a crowd.'

'Do you mean what I think you mean?' he questioned.

'Of course I do,' she purred, 'you were so fantastic last night I don't mind sharing.'

'Hang on a minute,' Conrad said, and the 'phone was muffled. She waited patiently and soon his voice came back full of interest – 'Come right up baby, we'll be waiting.'

She hung up smiling and made her way leisurely to the powder room, where for the next twenty minutes she touched up her make-up and re-arranged her hair so that it fell around her shoulders thick and shiny. She looked very gorgeous, young, sexy and pretty. Her figure was shown off to its best advantage in the low cut black dress she was wearing.

A half hour had passed by the time she finally knocked on the door of his suite and he answered almost immediately – wearing a livid green and orange striped bathrobe. 'Where the hell have you been?' he demanded.

She smiled apologetically, she knew she looked great. She walked into the living-room and sat down, crossing her legs carefully to be sure there was the maximum amount of thigh showing.

'I'm so sorry,' she said, 'I know you're going to think I'm terrible. But what I said on the 'phone about a threesome and everything. Well, I'm sorry but I just can't.'

He stared at her disbelievingly. 'You can't?' he said thickly.

She shook her head slowly fluttering long black eyelashes. 'I guess I wanted to see you again so much, I just said it – but really, it's not my scene.'

'It's not your scene,' he repeated blankly.

'No,' she licked her lips, crossed her legs the other way and waited.

'Look baby,' he said at last. 'You called me while I was balling this chick,' he indicated the bedroom, 'you called me up right in the middle. Nobody asked you to – but there you were on the 'phone – asking, and I mean asking, to join us. So what happens – you get me all hot over the idea of a scene – I stop halfway with this other broad – wait a goddam half hour and then you mince in here saying you can't make it.' His voice had been rising excitedly and now he was almost screaming!

She stood up – 'What can I say?' She walked over to him and put her hand on his arm. 'I was drunk last night, but in spite of that I remembered last night as something special. Now I'm sober and can I help it if I don't want to share you?'

He looked at her admiringly. 'You're a smart little cookie, I suppose you want me to get rid of –' he gestured towards the bedroom.

She kissed him, pressing herself up against him hard, 'That's the general idea.'

He pushed her away. 'All right baby – but don't think you're fooling me, because I'm hip to exactly what you're doing. You happen to be a lot prettier than her, so I'll pay her off. Is that what you want?'

She looked at him wide-eyed. 'I don't know what you're talking about,' she said, 'do whatever you want, I'll still be available tomorrow night, I can always go now.'

His eyes swept over her body – 'No, you stay, wait in the bathroom.'

She smiled and walked obediently into the bathroom which was in the hall. He kept her waiting about five minutes and she heard a shrieky female voice and then a door slammed. Eventually he threw open the bathroom door – he had discarded his vibrant bathrobe and stood there with nothing but his suntan and a hard on. 'Let's go baby,' he said, 'I just had to give that broad fifty bucks, so you'd better make it worth my while!'

David parked the car in the garage and let himself into the house. It was strangely quiet, and he supposed Linda had gone to bed early. He made his way upstairs and looked in on the children who both slept peacefully. Jane woke up and sleepily requested a glass of water. He got it for her and she threw her arms around his neck and said 'I love you Daddy'. He settled her down and went into the main bedroom. It was empty. He was mildly surprised. Where on earth was Linda? He knew the rest of the house was deserted. She must have gone to a movie or something, but it was most unlike her.

He checked through the window and saw her car was not in the drive, and then he looked around for a note – no note. He went along to Anna's room and knocked. The maid came to the door – she was clutching her transparent nylon nightdress around her and she featured a heavy black moustache.

'Where's Mrs. Cooper?' he questioned.

'She went out maybe eight o'clock,' said Anna. Her English was not too good, and she didn't volunteer any further information.

'Did she say where she was going?'

'No.'

'What time she would be back?'

'No.'

The conversation was finished.

He went back to the bedroom, showered and fell asleep reading the papers on the bed.

That was how Linda found him when she came in. She was surprised, he had said twelve o'clock and he was always later than he said he would be.

Fortunately he was asleep, as her make-up was all off and her hair a mess and she knew if he saw her he would surmise something. She made it into the bathroom quickly and got out of her clothes and into a robe; at least if he woke up now it wouldn't matter. She ran a bath. David awoke. 'Where the hell have you been?' he said.

'I went to a movie, where were you?'

'You know where I was. The movies get out a quarter to eleven – where have you been for the last hour?'

'I suppose you were with Phillip,' said Linda, ignoring his question to her.

'Yes – you know I was with Phillip.'

'Well, I was with Phillip too.'

He stared at her blankly. 'What are you talking about?'

'I was with Phillip as much as you were with Phillip.'

'Have you been drinking?'

'No, David, I haven't been drinking. I called the Abbottson house after speaking to you earlier, and while I was talking to Mary, Phillip came in and he knew nothing about a meeting with you.'

'Oh,' David thought quickly, 'yes, things were a bit of a mess. I thought Phillip was coming back later, but then I realized he had said he couldn't so then I had to take those people from out of town, out to dinner.'

She raised an eyebrow at him – 'But you just said you were with Phillip.'

'Yes – well that was because I knew you wouldn't understand.'

'You were right, I don't understand. Now please can I take a bath?'

'Oh, you're so ridiculous, Linda,' his voice was becoming louder – 'Look, I've been home for hours. I took these three men to Carlo's and I ran into Jay and Lori Grossman. Now do you believe me? They want us to have dinner with them tomorrow, and I said it was all right. Now you can ask them who I was with. O.K.?'

She was surprised, maybe he was telling the truth. 'Oh all right,' she said wearily.

He stalked back into the bedroom. She took her bath. Their thoughts were on separate planes. Neither of them really wanted to get involved in long discussions about who had been where as it was dangerous ground and they could end up getting found out themselves.

She came to bed. He thought how pretty she looked. She was wearing a long pink silk nightdress that clung seductively to her.

He broke the silence. 'Where would you like to eat tomorrow?'

She was non-commital, 'I don't mind.'

'Jay says Lori wants to go to the Savoy Grill – a bit conventional but I suppose as they are visitors here we should oblige.'

'Yes, I suppose so.' She turned out the light on her side of the bed and lay with her back towards him.

'What's new with the children?'

'Oh nothing much.'

He lit a cigarette. 'I'm not tired,' he remarked.

'Why don't you read? There's that book back there that you started about three months ago.'

'I don't feel like reading.'

'Well, turn your light off and go to sleep then.'

'That's a pretty nightdress, is that new?'

'No, I've been wearing it for the past two years,' she said patiently.

He leaned over and cupped her left breast with his hand. She shrank away immediately.

Oh, God no, she thought, not tonight – please God not tonight. After all those nights I've lain here and ached for him he couldn't possibly pick tonight.

He lounged across the bed after her. 'What's the matter?'

'Nothing,' she forced herself to turn around and face him.

Fortunately he took her quickly. He had long ago given up preliminaries with her. The sexual act with him gave her absolutely no pleasure, she felt vacant and used. She wondered vaguely if all men became like this after you married them. In courting days, anxious to please, thrilled to bits if they got to fondle you for half-an-hour. But after the marriage – a quick lay and that was that.

'That was marvellous,' he said, 'how was it for you?'

She simulated pleasure. 'Marvellous,' she repeated his adjective unable to think of anything else to say.

He turned the light out. 'Goodnight.'

68

She squeezed her eyes shut to keep in the tears, 'Good-night.'

He lay there and thought about what a bitch Claudia was.

She lay there and thought about how virile and sensitive Paul was.

Finally, they both fell asleep.

CHAPTER TEN

'I want to stay the night,' Claudia said, stretching languorously.

Conrad was on the 'phone to room service. He sat on the side of the bed, rolls of suntanned flesh around his middle, bald head shining slightly with sweat.

'This is Mr. Lee, suite 206 – send me up six pieces of lightly buttered toast spread with caviar – and the best stuff I mean. Also a bucket of ice, a glass of milk and a dish of chocolate ice cream,' he glanced over at Claudia – 'You want anything, baby?'

She shook her head.

He spoke into the 'phone again, 'Also some chocolate cake and some cream – a jug of cream. O.K., that's all.'

'I'm going to stay the night,' Claudia announced.

'What do you want to do that for?'

''Cos I want to go to the studio with you tomorrow like you promised, I'm not letting you out of my sight!'

He laughed, 'Baby, you're too much! I've been married three times and I thought I knew broads pretty well, but you're something else!'

She laughed too, throwing her head back so that her hair spread out around her, 'Wouldn't you sooner I was honest?' she asked. 'I'm not some naïve little bit, you know. I dig you, I think you're the end. But, also, I don't see why you shouldn't help me.'

'I haven't promised you anything.'

'Oh yes you have, you've promised me a test.'

69

'So I've promised you a test. So what if you're lousy?'

'I won't be lousy,' she smiled, 'I may not be able to act but I photograph like a dream! And in the sort of movie you're making I'm sure you can find something for me.'

There was a discreet knock on the bedroom door. 'Your order is here, sir,' a voice said.

Conrad lumbered off the bed and reached for a paisley silk dressing-gown.

God – you're old and fat, Claudia thought. 'I love your dressing-gown, darling,' she purred.

'Simpsons,' he said, pleased. He grabbed some change off the dressing-table and disappeared into the other room.

Claudia rolled across the bed twining herself round in the sheet.

'I'm going to get in his damn movie if it kills me,' she muttered to herself. 'I haven't screwed that for nothing!'

He came back into the bedroom munching on a piece of toast. 'This is lousy caviar – you want to go out somewhere?'

'What time is it?' she asked surprised.

He consulted a large gold watch. 'One-thirty – what's open?'

She thought quickly if they went out she wanted to be sure that she came back to the hotel with him after. She was determined to stick with him until he got her a test.

'All the clubs stay open till around four,' she said, 'and we can stop by my apartment so I can get some clothes to wear to the studio tomorrow. Great idea.' She jumped out of bed.

He studied her figure. 'You know you really have a beautiful body, how would you feel about appearing on the screen nude?'

'I hadn't really thought about it.'

'Think about it. There's a part you might be right for.

'So test me.'

They went to a new discotheque – Charlie Browns. It was jammed but they were squeezed on to an already full table due to the fact that Conrad slipped the head waiter five pounds.

The records were so loud you couldn't hear yourself speak and on the tiny dance floor couples were jammed together frantically shaking and surging and having a ball. There was a scattering of well known people, a lot of girls in mad gear with long straight hair and long straight fringes covering half their faces, and a few representatives of the latest swinging pop groups sporting hair almost as long as the girls.

It was very dark.

At their table there was a photographer Claudia knew. She greeted him with a kiss and introduced him to Conrad. He was with one of the top models of the moment, a tall slim girl who photographed out of this world.

Claudia couldn't sit still, the music swept over her in a great wave of loudness and beat.

'Can you shake?' she asked Conrad.

'Can I what?'

'Shake, dance, hustle,' she screamed at him to be heard above the noise.

They struggled to the dance floor, where Claudia broke loose in mad wild sinuous gyrations. Conrad just sort of stood there jiggling about. It was hot and the sweat started to trickle down Conrad's bald head. God you think you're a swinger, Claudia thought, look at you making a fool of yourself – don't you know you're too old to do this. She said 'Darling, you're a peachy dancer!'

'Sweetie pie!' The voice was unmistakable. Right beside them on the dance floor was Shirley, complete with the Hon. Jeremy. 'Where's your divine boy-friend?'

Claudia smiled. 'Thought you were going to Windsor,' she yelled.

'Well, sweetie, we did, but it was absolutely too dreadful. I mean it was almost empty. Can you imagine anything more ghastly?'

The Hon. Jeremy nodded vehement agreement.

By this time Conrad was sweating profusely. 'Let's sit down,' he said weakly.

'Sweetie, we will come over in a minute. Where are you sitting?'

Claudia smiled and waved pretending she hadn't heard. She didn't relish the thought of being stuck with Shirley and Jeremy again.

When they got back to their table it was even more crowded, and there was a great squeezing up of people to make room for them.

The model girl said to Conrad, 'I adored your last film. Will you be making your new one in this country?'

The photographer asked Claudia to dance. She accepted,

71

not too eager to leave the skinny bird chatting up Conrad, but anxious to dance again, and Giles the photographer was a wild dancer.

Claudia had had a short affair with him at one time, but they had decided it was much more fun to be mates. They were too much of a kind to be lovers. Occasionally, if one or the other was at a loose end they would call each other and spend an evening together and if they felt like it end up in bed. But it was purely a brother and sister relationship with a little sex thrown in. Giles was very good looking in a dark, almost Spanish way. Women were mad for him and his services as a fashion and society photographer were in demand.

'Who's the father figure?' he asked cynically. 'Cindy say's he's a big Hollywood mogul and I think she fancies big Hollywood moguls.'

'Well, tell her to keep her false nails off this one, he's already been bagged!'

They did a ritual dance together – him standing very still and giving rhythmic sexy twitches and she almost bumping and grinding before him. 'Fancy a bit of pot?' he asked conversationally.

She glanced over at their table, some more people had joined it and Conrad seemed quite happy ordering drinks and talking loudly with a lot of arm waving.

'Yeah, great idea,' she said.

They slipped off the dance floor and out on to a balcony that extended along one half of the club. It was windy and surprisingly quiet as the windows and doors from the club were all soundproofed.

Giles lit one cigarette and they took it in turn to drag deeply on it.

'I've got to get in the right frame of mind to screw that bag of bones,' he said. 'We're doing a big layout for *Vogue* and I want to have the right atmosphere between us. Christ, I tell you it's like banging a skeleton!'

They both giggled. 'Lots of luck,' laughed Claudia, 'how would you like mine? Attractive, isn't he?'

'I'd suggest a foursome,' said Giles, 'but I know we'd only end up doing it to each other, so what's the use.'

They both collapsed in gales of laughter at this, then Claudia said, 'C'mon, we'd better get back inside.'

72

'What's the scene?' Giles asked. 'You going to become a big movie starlet?'

'Star – baby – star.'

They walked back into the noise and heat and rejoined their table. Cindy was listening attentively as Conrad told a long boring story about how he first arrived in America at the age of fourteen. Shirley and the Hon. Jeremy had also joined the table.

'Sweetie – what a fascinating man!' gasped Shirley – 'Such a history.'

'Hello, Giles poppet.'

'Hello, Shirley – how's business?'

'Business?'

He laughed. 'Forget it baby.'

'I say, old man,' stammered Jeremy, 'liked those photos you did of Shirley – jolly fine set.'

'Well. I'm a jolly fine photographer.'

Claudia and Giles both fell about at that and then Claudia decided it was about time she came between Cindy's adoring gaze and Conrad. She snaked her arm around his neck and whispered something in his ear – he looked surprised. 'Here?' he said, 'Now?'

She giggled. 'No one will see, want me to?'

He laughed hoarsely. 'You're a wild broad, save it for later, huh?'

For some obscure reason Conrad ordered champagne for the whole table, and everyone proceeded to get well and truly loaded.

'I'm going to throw a big party tomorrow night,' said Conrad.

Claudia was delighted – 'For me, darling?'

'Yeah for you – anyone – you're all invited.'

'Oh goodie – how super,' trilled Shirley – 'where and what time, sweetie?'

'Make it at my hotel – Plaza Carlton – I'll take over a big room there – about ten o'clock.'

'Crazy,' said Claudia, 'did everybody hear that – to-morrow at ten.' She kissed Conrad's ear. 'I'm just going to the loo – be right back.' She threaded her way through the crowded tables to reception. 'I want to make a quick 'phone call,' she said to the girl there.

'Go ahead,' said the girl passing over the house 'phone.

It was after three o'clock. She dialled the number slowly,

73

a strange smile playing around her lips. A sleepy male voice answered the 'phone. 'Hello, David darling,' she whispered, 'I'm having a great time, how about you?'

She hung up immediately. 'Just letting my husband know everything's cool,' she said to the surprised girl and swept back inside.

Waking up the next morning was not too much fun. Seeing Conrad asleep beside her like a discontented slug made her stomach turn. Her head felt heavy and her skin like much used parchment. She made it to the bathroom and took an icy cold shower. It was absolutely freezing agony, but the after effects were worth it.

They had not returned to Conrad's hotel earlier that morning but instead had ended up in her flat.

After the shower she dressed carefully, and did a meticulous make-up, all ready to accompany Conrad to the studio. Then she made some coffee and finally shook him. He woke up badly. Much coughing and foul sounds in his throat, blood-shot eyes, bad breath and B.O.

'Christ, what time is it?' he muttered, the universal cry of people waking up in other people's apartments.

'It's just ten o'clock.' She handed him some coffee.

'Where's the 'phone?'

She groped around under the bed, where she had placed the phone off the hook.

He called his secretary and issued a list of instructions. 'I've got to get back to the hotel and get changed,' he said, struggling into his clothes.

'I'm coming with you.'

'Oh c'mon baby – what for?'

'For my test you promised me.'

He stared at her. 'I'm not going to forget your damn test – but it can't be done just like that, today, it's got to be set up.'

'So I'll come with you while you set it up.'

He shook his head. 'You don't give up, do you.' He picked up the phone and called his secretary again. 'Listen, I want a test fixed for a Miss Claudia –' he looked at her blankly –

'Parker,' she said quickly.

'Parker. Fix it up as soon as possible, her agent will call you later today to get the details.'

He hung up. 'O.K. baby?'

She kissed him. 'O.K. baby, listen, you haven't forgotten the party tonight.'

'Party?'

'Yes, don't you remember you asked a whole group of people to a party tonight at your hotel.'

'Oh yeah – that's right, I'll get it in hand. All right baby, see you later then.'

'Yes, I'll come by a couple of hours early in case you need anything.'

'The way I feel right now I won't need anything – but you never know.' He gave a ribald laugh and left.

CHAPTER ELEVEN

Linda 'phoned Paul at work as soon as the children had gone off to school and David to the office.

He was anxious to see her.

'I can't manage it,' she said.

He was most persuasive and eventually she agreed to meet him during his lunch hour. It was a crisp sunny day and they met in Green Park. She had never seen him in a suit before and it didn't look quite right somehow. She decided it was because it was ready made and ready made suits always manage to be just that little bit wrong.

They strolled along hand in hand but Linda didn't feel easy. She felt over-dressed in her matching coat and hat and crocodile shoes and bag. She knew she looked all wrong strolling hand in hand with Paul Bedford in Green Park. It wasn't that she felt old, or at least older than him – but she felt in spite of the fact that she didn't want to feel that way – she felt she was slumming.

'What's on your mind?' he asked. 'Something bothering you?'

'Oh, I don't know, Paul. You know this is all wrong. I'm not the sort of woman that can get involved in an affaire.

I have my children and my home and I feel I must keep trying with my husband. It must be partly my fault that things have gone so wrong. I can't just give up and become involved with you. That's no answer at all.'

'What's the matter, Linda? Are you frightened of losing your security if David finds out?'

'No, I'm frightened of losing my self-respect.'

They walked in silence for a while and then he said, 'What are you trying to say?'

'I'm trying to say that I can't lead two lives, I want to stop it now before it goes any further.'

His voice sounded weak. 'Don't leave me now that I've found you. I've been waiting and hoping to meet someone like you. You're a warm person, I need a warm person, I won't make any demands on you, just to see you when you're free.'

'It's not enough for either of us, I don't want to see you again.'

His mood changed. 'You're like all the others. I should have known you're just a hard bitch at heart, you're frightened of losing all your home comforts. Women have hearts like bloody adding machines. Look at Margarethe – dropped me for my father just because he had a few bob. My bloody mother killed herself to get away from him, and my bloody sister took off one day and vanished to get away from him, but then what happens? My girl friend marries him.'

'I'm sorry, Paul – but I'm not going to be a substitute for your mother, sister, or Margarethe. I'm too old for you. Forget the past and go and find someone you can be happy with.'

'Is that what you want?'

'That's what I want.'

He sneered at her, 'Well you were a bloody easy lay – and not bad for an old bird.'

She turned and started to walk quickly away.

'Who's going to stuff your crumpet now?' he yelled after her.

She felt the colour rise in her face, and she started to run, not stopping until she reached her car. She leaped in and started the car. He was nowhere in sight. She drove home, cold tears running down her face all the way.

The Grossmans were sitting in the bar of their hotel, Lori cool in pale lilac chiffon, silver hair swept back in elaborate curls, neckline plunging to show off two satin smooth white breasts.

Jay was wearing a well-cut black suit with a button down collar and a black knit tie. They made an extremely good-looking couple.

The Coopers arrived to meet them exactly on time. Linda was wearing a black silk dress and pale beige mink stole, her short auburn hair rather severe but very chic. David, conventional in a midnight-blue suit, white shirt, blue tie and big sapphire cuff-links.

They all had a drink and then moved on to the Savoy Grill.

Jay enlivened the evening with amusing tales about Hollywood. David chatted amicably about business and politics. The two women were mostly silent. Lori was obviously disappointed that Princess Margaret wasn't there. She complained about the lack of ice and checked her make-up a lot.

Jay finally said, 'For Christ sake stop looking in the mirror, we all know you're beautful, it's the reason I married you, isn't it?'

She pouted a lot after that.

When they were on the coffee, Jay said, 'Hey – how about dropping by the party Conrad's giving tonight, we promised we would.'

'I'm really feeling a bit tired,' Linda said, 'you know it was the children's first day at school, and what with all the preparation, I'm rather exhausted.'

'Oh, come on, Linda,' said David jovially. He was feeling rather pleased with himself due to the fact that he had avoided getting in touch with Claudia all day. Little tramp, teach her a lesson. And how about that 'phoning him up in the middle of the night to make him jealous. He would show her, she would have to come begging to be forgiven.

'Yes, Linda, you must come,' said Jay. 'It will be a laugh, I can promise you that.'

'Oh all right.'

She accompanied Lori to the ladies' room, where between applying powder rouge, Lori drawled, 'That son of a bitch thinks I'm a damn idiot. He'll find out who's the idiot when I get half of everything he's got.'

'I beg your pardon?' said Linda politely.

'It's California law – I know it's California law.' At that Lori sank into silence, carefully applying another coat of lip gloss.

The party was in full swing when they arrived. There were sixty or seventy people there already and more arriving all the time. Huge buffets of good food covered one side of the room, and there were three bars strategically placed and a swinging six-piece group to which people were dancing.

They pushed their way through to the nearest bar and ordered drinks. Jay appeared to know quite a few people and he introduced everybody and soon David and Linda were involved with different groups chatting away.

'Come with me to find Conrad,' Jay said to Linda 'I must at least let him know I put up an appearance.'

They found Conrad sitting at a table eating chocolate ice cream and drinking straight bourbon. Claudia was by his side – wearing a bright red ruffled dress and a lot of fake diamonds.

Conrad gave genial greetings and invited them to sit down, moving two other people to do so.

'You remember Mrs. Cooper – Linda,' Jay said.

'Sure, sure, what do you think of the party? I know how to do these things right, huh?'

'You certainly do,' Jay said admiringly.

'Hallo, Mrs. Cooper,' Claudia said, slurring her words slightly, she had been drinking steadily for several hours. 'Is Mr. Cooper about?'

'Why yes,' said Linda. 'Did you want to see him about something?'

'Yes, as a matter of fact I did.' She knocked a glass down on the table accidentally, the dark alcohol making a splashy stain on the tablecloth. 'I want to tell him what he can do with his bloody Beauty Maid campaign. Stuff it up his arse – that's what he can do with it,' she hiccoughed.

Linda stared at her coolly. 'I'll see he gets the message, dear,' she said and turned to talk to Jay.

Claudia stood up from the table. 'I think I'll give him the bloody message myself,' she said, and weaved unsteadily off.

'Well,' Linda was startled, 'what's the matter with her?'

78

Jay shrugged. 'I don't know. What's with your girl-friend Con?'

Conrad laughed – 'Oh, she's a cuke. I've promised her a bit in the movie and it's gone to her head.'

'What bit?'

'I thought it would be a cute idea to have a semi-naked broad standing beside the credits, sort of torn slave dress jazz. This kid's got a great body – and if she photographs O.K. we'll use her. O.K.?'

'Fine,' said Jay with a smile. 'Sounds like it has a lot of class!'

Linda arose from the table. 'Excuse me a minute,' she said. She walked hesitantly around the room looking for David, she couldn't see the drunken girl or him. She sighed, it was probably nothing, the girl was drunk.

She saw Lori surrounded by a group of admiring males. She went over. Lori was saying, 'Well where we come from, we just don't have any problem with negroes. They know their place and keep it. Why, some of my best maids were coloured.'

'Have you seen David?' Linda asked.

'Yeah,' she hardly glanced at Linda. 'He went out on the terrace.'

It's stupid, Linda thought, I shouldn't be tracking him down like this, it's childish. She made her way on to the terrace and found it deserted.

Just as she was leaving she heard a low throaty chuckle, she looked again and saw over in the corner a couple in a close embrace.

She backed into the shadows and edged closer. The girl was pulling his head down to her breast which was popping out of the top of her dress, she was fondling him intimately.

'You're the craziest, Claudia,' he muttered, 'the best ever.' Now he was pulling her dress right down so it hung around her waist. 'I missed you so much, one night without having you was hell.'

Shocked and sickened, Linda backed away. They hadn't seen her. Dazed, she wandered back into the main room. She was heading for the door when Jay appeared and grabbed her arm. 'What's the matter, you look terrible, what happened?'

She looked at him with unseeing eyes. 'I've got to get out

79

of here,' she mumbled, pushing his arm away and continuing to make for the door.

He caught hold of her arm again firmly and steered her to the nearest bar.

'The lady wants a large brandy, and fast,' he said. 'Now tell me what the hell has happened, Linda.' He took her hand and held it tight. 'Tell me,' he said in a softer voice.

She looked at him, her eyes were full of shock. 'I suspected he played around – maybe – once in a blue moon, up in Manchester or something – but this . . . With me right here. It's horrible.'

The waiter brought the brandy and she took large gulps. 'I – I was looking for David. I wanted to warn him about that drunk tart. Lori said he was on the terrace. I went there and he was there with her, they were necking – she had half her dress off, they were saying these things to each other. . . .'

'Oh God!' said Jay, 'that stupid son of a bitch. Look – I mean the girl was drunk, maybe he was trying to get rid of her.'

Linda's eyes were scornful. 'With words like – one night without having you was hell.'

'What do you want to do?' asked Jay. 'Shall I take you home?'

She shook her head. 'What can I do? This is it for me. I can't go on after this. I'm finished with him. I want to divorce him. I hate him.' Her voice shook. 'I want to go home but I can't, I can't even speak to him again. What can I do?'

'Look – it's no good making decisions while you're upset. Let me take you home. I'll come straight back and talk to David, tell him not to go home tonight.'

She laughed bitterly – 'Tell him not to ever come home again. Tell him to go off with his 'best ever' little slut. Tell him he can do what he wants – 'cos I don't care any more, I'm having nothing to do with him any more, I'm through.' She took another large gulp of brandy. 'I'm going to start crying in a minute – please get me out of here.'

They got a taxi outside the hotel. Linda was worried that either Lori or David would miss them and that maybe David would come home, but Jay reassured her, 'I'll be back within an hour and if he does miss you he'll just be looking round. As for Lori, she won't even know I'm gone.'

80

'Oh Jay,' Linda sighed, 'I'm so embarrassed, dragging you away from the party and everything. The whole situation is so sordid and awful.'

'Don't be embarrassed,' he took her hand comfortingly. 'If it's any solace I was involved in exactly the same situation myself. In Hollywood at a real swinging party, my first wife Jenny vanished, I searched all over and eventually found her in bed with the host. So you see I do understand.'

'What did you do?'

'I was a shmuck, I gave her another chance, came home early one day and found her banging the delivery boy.'

They sat in silence for a while, then Jay said, 'I suppose for some people one woman or man is enough – but not for any of the people I know. I guess one gets what one deserves out of life. I've been married three times – each time to a beautiful girl with about as much thinking power as a rabbit. It must be a sickness with me – I marry stupid dumb beautiful broads.'

Linda hesitated. 'I – I was unfaithful to David this week. The first time in eleven years of marriage. I'm so ashamed about it now. It was with a boy – a twenty-year-old boy – I don't know why . . .' She tailed off, 'David hadn't touched me in months, we were so far apart, he was never home. It just happened. I suppose I'm as guilty as he is.'

'Listen – never feel guilty. What good can that do? Sleep on things, and see how you feel in the morning. You've got young children, don't make any hasty decisions.'

The taxi arrived at the house.

'Goodnight, Jay – thank you for everything.'

'Linda, I'll call you tomorrow, rest easy – it will be all right.'

Claudia found David in a group with Lori. She edged quietly up behind him and pressing her body against his back she covered his eyes with her hands and said in a Marilyn Monroe type voice, 'Guess who, baby!'

There was no mistaking that body. He was surprised, and suddenly sharply excited. She had the most incredible effect on him, he just had to know she was there to want her. He turned slowly, eyes looking around to see if Linda was anywhere about. She wasn't.

'Hello, Claudia.'

'Hello, Claudia,' she mimicked his voice. 'Don't I get

a better greeting than that? By the way, you can stuff your beauty Maid Campaign up your arse, Cha cha cha!'

The group he had been standing with were all listening interestedly, including Lori.

He took Claudia firmly by the arm, bruising her flesh. 'Let's go and find Linda,' he said, walking off and pulling her with him.

'Let's go find Linda!' she said incredulously. 'You've got to be joking!'

He marched her on to the terrace, finding a deserted dark corner. As soon as he let go of her she wound her arms around his neck and kissed him. 'Did you miss me?' she whispered. 'I was going to be so mad at you, but I couldn't,' she giggled, 'I'm smashed, you know.'

'You're a little bitch, leaving me sitting in that restaurant, 'phoning up in the middle of the night. *You* were going to be mad, what about me?'

She nibbled his ear, rubbing her body against him.

Her dress was held up by two thin shoulder straps, he peeled them off, pulling her dress down to her waist. She wore nothing underneath and she guided his mouth to her breasts.

All sense of reason was gone. He was with Claudia and had to have her, it didn't matter that they were on a public terrace, that his wife was somewhere around, that anybody could appear. It was dark. He pushed her down on to the cold concrete ground and lifted her skirt, she wore no panties and she was giggling. He took her quickly, it was all over in a minute. 'Christ!' he mutttered. 'Christ!'

She lay there still giggling, her dress just a bunch around her waist. He pulled her up, looking around, relieved to see that no one had come out. She was unconcerned.

'We've got to go back inside separately,' he said.

'Screw you!' she replied.

'You just did.' He straightened his tie and wiped a handkerchief around his face to remove all traces of lipstick and make up. 'Listen, I'll phone you tomorrow. I'll get away early from the office and come over. I've got a surprise for you.'

'You've always got a surprise for me. You're the man with the permanent hard on!' she laughed. 'What a title for a television series – I can see it now – The Man With The Permanent Hard On – starring Dick Hampton!'

He kissed her – 'You go in first – go straight to the ladies' room, you look a mess.'

'Thank you, kind sir. Are you sure you're finished with me?'

'Go on, be a good girl, I'll try to 'phone you later.'

She stuck out her tongue at him – waggling it obscenely, and then sauntered off through the french windows completely at ease.

He took a deep breath – what a girl! After a safe five minutes he followed her in. The party was still in full swing. He grabbed a drink from a passing waiter and started to look around for Linda. This was becoming a dangerous habit, bumping into Claudia at parties.

He observed Lori dancing with a seedy, fairly well known actor. She was moving her hips in steady bumps and grinds and she smiled coolly at him. She certainly knew how to move. He edged closer.

'Seen Linda?' he said.

Lori looked deadpan – 'Last I saw of her she was heading towards the terrace looking for you.'

'The terrace?' he said, stunned.

'The terrace, honey,' she swayed away from him.

He started to look for Linda seriously. He ploughed his way across the room, through groups of people laughing and chatting. A girl grabbed his arm, she was thin and pretty and he remembered her as a friend of Claudia's from the restaurant.

'Hello, ducky,' she cooed, 'fancy seeing you here.'

'Hello,' he looked around for her spotty boyfriend.

'Oh, Jeremy's gone to fetch me another drink.' She didn't leave go of his arm. 'Super party – but I didn't expect you to be here.'

'Why not?' he said patiently, she was far too thin for him to find her attractive.

'Well, you know – I mean I know we're all very modern and everything, but you struck me as the jealous type.'

'What are you talking about?' He shook his arm free.

'Well after all – the party is being given by Conrad Lee for Claudia, and I shouldn't have thought you would come. I mean one shouldn't mix business with pleasure, should one? And you're obviously pleasure and he's obviously business,' she smiled blandly – 'here comes Jeremy with

83

my drink, see you again,' and she walked off to meet the approaching Jeremy.

'Bitch!' He stood there furious.

Claudia hadn't mentioned Lee or the fact that the party was for her. Bitch! Bitch! Bitch!

The quest for Linda was forgotten, and a new one for Claudia began. He wanted to get a few facts straight.

Jay arrived back at the party. He was thoughtful. It was a tricky situation to handle, telling another man he couldn't go home to his own wife. It could easily end in a punch on the nose. He saw David across the room talking to a girl.

He was an attractive man, big and dark and the ladies obviously fell for him. Lori had said she thought he was probably fantastic in bed, but from talking to Linda it didn't sound that way. Lori had a habit of thinking most men were fantastic in bed, her way of letting Jay know that she didn't think he was. He approached David quickly, best to get it over with fast. He told him the situation. David was suitably flattened. He tried to deny it but when Jay told him word for word what Linda had told him, he was forced to admit it.

'You're an idiot,' Jay said. 'You've got a great wife, if you want to screw around why do it under her nose?'

'What is she going to do?'

'She mentioned divorce.'

'She can't talk like that, she's got no proof. So I kissed a girl at a party, what does that prove? I'm going home, I'm not going to be shut out of my own home.'

Jay shrugged. 'I can't stop you, I can only offer advice. She's in a state of shock, going home tonight will only make things worse. If you wait until morning, I'm sure you'll both see things a hell of a lot clearer.'

'I'm going home. I know Linda, she's upset but I can explain to her.'

Jay glared at him. 'I promised Linda that you'd stay away tonight.'

David glared back. 'Well, that's tough because I'm going home now.'

They held the glare a few moments and then Jay said, 'Goodnight, shmuck, don't forget to say goodnight to your girl-friend, you'll probably find her kissing Conrad's arse.'

On that note they parted company.

CHAPTER TWELVE

When David arrived at his house and put his key in the front door it wouldn't open. He lit a match to make sure he was using the right key, but although it turned smoothly, the door remained tight shut. Realization dawned, Linda had bolted it from the inside. He went around to the back door, but that was also tightly barred. A strong choked anger rose in him. He returned to the front door and pressed his finger firmly down on the bell push. The jangly sound of the buzzer was loud and insistent. There was no response. He tried it again, this time leaving his finger there for several minutes. A light went on in the upstairs window, it was the maid's room. He waited impatiently for her to come down and let him in, but nothing happened and after a while her light went out again.

He was furious – Linda was obviously up, and had told Anna to ignore the bell. He kicked savagely at the door but only succeeded in hurting his foot. This is incredible, he thought, who the hell does she think the bloody house belongs to!

'Listen, Linda,' he shouted, 'don't be such a fool – open the door or I'm going for the police.'

The house loomed still and dark before him. What to do? He banged on the door with his fists – nothing. He leaned on the bell push again – nothing. Then, faintly, from upstairs, there floated down the sound of a child crying. He stood there, undecided about what to do. He felt guilty about waking the children, but after all, it was really Linda's fault for not letting him in. He pushed the bell firmly and insistently for one final time and to his surprise the bolts were pushed back and the door opened a few inches. He went to push it further open but it clanged to a shuddering stop – the chain was on.

Linda peered out at him, white-faced and angry. 'Go away, you make me sick.' Her voice sounded flat and tired.

'Oh come on, let me in, we'll talk about it, it was nothing – I was drunk.'

'I don't want to talk to you, I don't want to see you. Go back to your little scrubber and leave me alone.'

She slammed the door in his face.

He swore, hammered on the door and shouted, 'You'll be sorry, Linda. I'll bloody go away and I won't come back!'

She didn't return to the door. Furious, he strode back to his car, got in and started it viciously.

When David left the party, Jay 'phoned Linda and warned her. He then got hold of Lori who was dancing sexily with a swarthy-faced Ambassador and sat her down firmly in a corner.

'You saw David take that broad on to the terrace. What's with you, big mouth? Why did you tell Linda?'

She looked disinterested. 'I don't know what you're talking about, honey,' she drawled. 'Is something going on?'

'Yeah, something's going on,' he shrugged disgustedly. 'Are you really as drunk as you pretend to be?'

She looked sulky. 'You're so nasty to me, Jay, I don't know why I married you.'

'Would two mink coats, a chinchilla and a big house and pool jog your memory?'

She stood up, smoothing her hands down her body, ironing imaginary wrinkles in her dress. 'I'm going to dance again, you interrupted me before – that was a very sweet important guy I was dancing with.'

She walked off, beautiful, cool. Jay shook his head in despair, she was an idiot or a bitch or a clever combination of both.

The noise at the table that Conrad and his group were sitting at was becoming progressively louder. Shrieks of drunken laughter, spilt drinks, Claudia climbing on the table and dancing, with the men all peering up her skirt, becoming aware of the fact that she had no panties on. Egged on with screams of drunken encouragement, she started to peel her dress off.

Jay viewed the scene, he was horribly sober, they all seemed to be behaving like a bunch of wild monkeys. He felt disgusted.

A large crowd was gathering round the table goggle-eyed

at Claudia's free show. The foreign Ambassador rushed over with Lori. It was a fast strip tease, as Claudia only had her dress to take off. She threw it off, kicking it from the table, and then proceeded to dance to the music of a slow hand clap from the crowd. Her body glistened proudly and the men in the crowd pressed closer and closer while the women, suddenly jealous at such perfection, started to try and move them away.

A very harassed-looking man in pin-stripe trousers and black jacket pushed his way towards the table. He represented the management, shocked and horrified he approached Conrad, who waved him drunkenly away. 'We shall have to call the police unless this – this – woman gets dressed at once.'

Claudia stuck her tongue out at him, the only part of her that hadn't been exposed to public view.

Eventually of course the police arrived, they wrapped Claudia in a blanket, hauled her off to the police station and booked her for indecent exposure.

The next morning it was headlines. Claudia was a star for the day that is. She was photographed and quoted, and Conrad immediatetly cashed in on her wave of publicity and announced that she would be appearing in his new film. He contacted her agent and signed her for two days' work at £80 per day.

She was delighted. She returned from the police station at lunch time, triumphant. She gave a press reception, posed for countless more pictures, and then was taken off to the studio in a chauffered car for make-up and hair tests. She didn't see Conrad, efficient young men took over. She was pleased, he had served his immediate purpose, and she hers. When she returned from the studio in the evening, David was propped outside her front door. Sober and giddy with her sudden success he didn't look so good to her. 'What do you want?' she said coldly, and then added with a burst of enthusiasm, 'Hey – did you see me in the papers today?'

He trailed her into the flat, and started immediately to mix a drink. She flitted around talking excitedly, forgetting her coldness of a moment before. After all, David did belong to someone else, and it was she he was coming to.

'I'm going to take you out to dinner tonight, where do you want to go?'

She laughed. 'Oh I see, all of a sudden I'm a star, and

you want to be seen with me! What about wifey tonight, then? Aren't you frightened one of her spies will see us?'

'You don't have to worry about her, I've left her.'

Silence hung heavy in the room until slowly Claudia walked over very close to him and kissed him hard. 'You've left her for me?'

'For you.' He ran his hands down her back enclosing them round her buttocks. 'I couldn't stand not being with you all the time any longer after last night and you doing that stupid strip with everybody ogling you. When I saw you in the paper this morning and I read what happened, I just knew we couldn't go on any longer unless it was together. So I told Linda, I said I wanted a divorce and here I am.'

She shook her head in disbelief. 'You really left her for me, isn't that wild!'

'I'm going to divorce her and marry you,' he said firmly.

She wandered round the room. 'I don't want to get married, but thanks for the thought anyway. Hey – baby, we can do what we want, go where we want. It's too much!'

He followed her round the room – 'Don't you understand, I said I'd marry you.'

She laughed. 'But I don't want you to. You don't have to.'

'But I want to,' he grabbed hold of her. She was wearing a clingy orange sweater, matching slacks and shiny white boots. She slipped away from him – 'Listen, baby – let's get clear on the subject. I don't – do not have, I repeat, any desire to make the wedding bells scene – so don't keep on making the offer like it's such a damn big deal. I don't want to marry you!' She was almost shouting, and sensing her mood, he dropped the subject.

'Where do you want to go?' he said. 'We can go anywhere you want.'

She stretched, cat-like, in her orange outfit. 'Oh I'm tired I don't feel like getting dressed and going out!'

He looked surprised – 'You're always complaining we never go anywhere – and now that we can go wherever you like – you don't want to go.'

She flopped in a chair, her legs thrown casually over the side – 'Ever heard the story of the kid that wanted some candy – moaned and cried and carried on till eventually it got candy – then ate so much it was sick?' She giggled, 'Get the message?'

'What the hell's the matter with you? Don't you understand what I've done for you today?'

She shrugged. 'For me? I should have thought it would have been for yourself. Where are you going to live?'

'I'm taking an apartment. I thought in the meantime I'd stay here with you, then we can move into the new place together.'

She studied her fingernails, admiring the pearly glow. 'Is it a penthouse?'

'Is what a penthouse?'

'The apartment you're taking.' There was a pause. 'Well, is it?'

'I don't know, what the hell does that matter? We'll find a penthouse if that's what you want.

She smiled at last, pleased and purry. 'Yes, that's what I want. Can I start looking tomorrow? It's going to be too crowded for the two of us here. She held out her arms to him, 'I'm sorry I've been bitchy, but it's been a busy day.'

He fell into her arms, and kissed her, feeling the familiar immediate desire rise in him.

She kissed him hard, running her tongue across his teeth and scratching the back of his neck with sharp nails. He started to reach for her body, but she pushed him away and leaped up. 'Not now, baby. Let's go to dinner and then think of it – we can come back home together. It will be a whole different scene.'

She switched on the record player and the sound of the 'Stones' filled the room. She danced around, throwing off her sweater and wriggling out of her slacks in time to the music. She wore a brief white bra and the shiny white boots.

He watched her, mesmerized. 'Why don't you ever wear pants?'

'Why spoil the line?' she laughed. 'Does it bother you? I've never had any complaints before!'

She vanished into the bathroom and he heard the sound of a bath running. He followed her in, she was bending over the bath, filling it with bubbles. She had discarded the bra, but the boots remained. He grabbed her from behind. She struggled weakly, half laughing. He tried to hold on to her and get out of his clothes at the same time, but she slipped and fell into the bath. By this time she was helpless with laughter and very wet and covered in bubbles, and she stuck her legs over the side of the bath with her boots still on. He undressed hurriedly and followed her into the bath. The water cascaded over the side.

'I think I'm going to like living here,' he said.

CHAPTER THIRTEEN

The sun was streaming into the bedroom and David couldn't sleep any longer. Claudia lay, sprawled beside him, taking up more than half her share of the bed. She claimed she couldn't sleep with the curtains drawn, which accounted for the fact that every morning the light woke him too early. He glanced at his watch, it was only half-past six and they hadn't got to bed until four. He felt tired and dreadful and hungover. It was no use getting up and drawing the curtains now, as he couldn't go back to sleep once he was awake.

The spacious bedroom was a mess. Claudia had a habit of stepping out of her clothes all over the place and just leaving them. Therefore one had to pick one's way through the debris in the mornings.

It's amazing, he thought, how my life has changed in such a short period of only six months.

The new dress he had bought her lay in a crumpled ball at the bottom of the bed. It was red pleated chiffon and she had seen it in a window in Bond Street and he had surprised her with it the next day. The surprise had cost him one-hundred and fifty pounds. He picked it up. She had spilt a glass of wine on it and there was a crumpled stain.

In the green marble bathroom leading off the bedroom the mess continued. She had not emptied the bath and it was filled with cold dirty water. Bottles of make-up and hair-brushes and perfumes were scattered everywhere. The sink was clogged with soap left to congeal beneath a dripping gold tap, and hair. Beneath the mess it was a beautiful apartment. A penthouse as she had wanted, in a new block of flats in Kensington. It cost far too much money a week, a fortune in fact. But Claudia loved it and didn't want to move.

He emptied the old water and picked up the bath towels on the floor. He really wished she could learn to be tidy, but it seemed impossible for her. With Linda, there had never been a thing out of place.

He went through a small marble lined, mirrored hallway to the kitchen. Here there were stale cups of half-drunk coffee, dirty dishes piled up, filled ashtrays creating a bad smoky atmosphere.

Fortunately it was Friday, which meant that they had a new cleaning woman starting. The last one had left in disgust when she found out they weren't married, leaving a cryptic note saying, 'I'm not used to such filth'. At first he thought she was referring to the state Claudia left things in, but the porter had told him what she really meant.

He made a cup of strong tea and managed to burn a couple of pieces of toast. Claudia had acquired a small yappy Yorkshire terrier which suddenly came bounding out, anxious to take a walk no doubt. It usually slept on the bed with them and would burrow beneath the covers at night. David hated it. He hated small dogs.

He left it sniffing around the kitchen and went into the huge open plan living-dining room. This was the pièce de résistance of the apartment, a beautiful spacious room, one wall completely glass, leading on to a landscaped patio, another wall marble and the rest of the wall space mirrored. The room was chaotic. They had people in for drinks before going out the previous evening, and half-empty glasses seemed to be all over the place. Overflowing ashtrays, spilled nuts, magazines, photographs of Claudia, cushions on the floor. Thank God it would all be cleared up today.

He went to the front door and collected the papers, extracting his *Times* and *Guardian* from amongst the various film and fashion magazines Claudia seemed to have delivered daily.

He drank his tea, it was too strong, ate his toast, it was burnt, and read the papers through bleary eyes. Soon it would be time to get dressed and go off to work.

Linda woke early. The sun was shining and it was a lovely day. She felt good.

At last she was starting to enjoy the selfish pleasures of

sleeping alone. Taking up the whole of the bed, waking and sleeping when she pleased, always being able to get into the bathroom.

It had been hard at first, the decision of getting a divorce terrible. She kept thinking of the children without a father. But the fact that David had moved out and set up home with Claudia had helped her to be strong; that he could do that was enough.

She found a good solicitor and put herself in his hands. It was quite simple really.

Today was the day, the day she was going to appear in court, stand calmly before a judge and state the facts. Her solicitor, a short stocky grey-haired man, would be by her side. An enquiry agent would be there to offer relevant information. Her counsel was tall and attractive and sympathetic, and they had all assured her it would go quite smoothly. It was undefended and clear cut.

She dressed, choosing her clothes carefully. A dark-brown neat suit, low-heeled shoes, not too much make-up. Surveying herself in the mirror, she thought she looked the part. An abandoned wife, sad, with feeling of courage.

The children were staying with her mother. She ate a solitary breakfast of boiled eggs and coffee, wishing that she hadn't sent them away wishing that their noisy laughter was filling the house.

However, after she was finished in court, she was going to leave by train and join them all for the week-end, and they would return to the house together on Monday. The house belonged to her now. Financial arrangements had been amicable. She got the house and fairly generous support for herself and the two children.

David visited the children every week-end either on Saturday or Sunday. Linda always managed to avoid seeing him. In fact, she hadn't seen him for three months and then it had been in her solicitor's office to make the financial settlement final.

She made only one stipulation about his seeing the children, and that was the fact that she didn't want them in Claudia's company at all. He didn't argue on that point.

She finished her coffee, soon it would be time to go to her solicitor's office and accompany him to court.

Claudia woke at eleven. There was someone ringing the

doorbell. She groped her way to the front door, struggling into a flimsy pink négligée covered in make-up stains.

A short squat woman stood facing her. 'I'm Mrs. Cobb,' she announced, 'the agency sent me.' She had red heavy hands and a scrubbed old face.

'Oh, come in, Mrs. Cobb,' Claudia said, stifling a yawn. 'I'm afraid it's a ghastly mess, but I'm sure you'll cope.'

She took her into the kitchen and gestured under the sink. 'You'll find everything you need under there. Excuse me if I leave you to it, I had a ghastly late night.'

Mrs. Cobb looked grimly around, and didn't say anything.

Claudia took a can of peaches from the fridge and tipped them into a dish – 'My breakfast,' she said with a bright smile and, stopping to collect the magazines and papers from the living-room, she went back into the bedroom.

Propped comfortably back in bed, she leafed idly through the papers, the *Daily Mail* being her favourite. It was the show page that interested her. She scanned it eagerly, looking, as usual, for any mention of Conrad Lee. She was delighted, today there was a whole article on the location of his film in Israel. It also stated that the company would be returning to England at the end of the week for studio work.

She made a big pencil ring around the article and 'phoned her agent on the shell-pink bedside telephone. She still had her two days' work to do on Conrad's film. Things had become rather complicated and the unit had gone on location before reaching Claudia's scenes. However the film company had given her agent constant promises that as soon as the unit returned she would be needed for her two days.

She gave her agent the good news and he promised to look into it immediately. She stretched languidly, the past few months since moving to the penthouse had been fun, although David was becoming a bit of a bore. The penthouse was too much! The most beautiful apartment. All her friends were very impressed. She had done lots of photographic assignments there, and she was always pleased when they appeared in various magazines – saying lovely young actress and model, Claudia Parker, relaxing in her penthouse apartment.

Giles was coming over at two o'clock to do a nude layout for a prominent American men's magazine. She hoped David would be working late, as he disliked Giles intensely, in

93

spite of the fact that he didn't even know she had had an affair with him. Anyway, if he knew she was doing a nude layout he would be furious, he was very stuffy that way. The American magazine was paying her and Giles a lot of money, and anyway she didn't mind showing off her body, after all, it was certainly worth showing.

She lounged back in bed, yawning. Soon it would be time to start preparing herself, until then she could relax.

David arrived at the office tired and bad-tempered. His secretary greeted him with a worried face. 'Oh, Mr. Cooper your uncle wants to see you at once, his secretary asked me to get you to go straight to his office as soon as you arrived.'

What now? Being summoned by Uncle Ralph was never good news. His uncle had been most disapproving about his split up with Linda. Divorce was a frowned-upon sin in the Jewish religion, and Uncle Ralph was very religious when it suited him.

He was sitting like a small, bald buzzard behind his desk in his early Victorian style office. His secretary, Penny, a wide-eyed blonde, ushered David in. He appraised her sexy long legs in her ultra short skirt. Trust Uncle Ralph to have the only good-looking secretary in the building.

'Good morning, David,' Uncle Ralph grunted. 'Sit down – sit down. Wanted to have a word with you about the Fulla Health Beans account.'

'We don't have it any more.'

'Exactly – exactly, that's what I wanted to talk to you about.' His uncle launched into a long lecture about the reason they had lost the account, which was because of David's unenthusiastic attitude lately, and the fact that he didn't seem in good health and was always tired. He hinted that perhaps the job was too much for him.

David listened carefully, dissecting every word Uncle Ralph said, because every word Uncle Ralph said always meant something else. What he was actually saying was – 'Don't come in here dragging your arse because you've been up with a hot piece all night. Either work or get the hell out.' He concluded the lecture with the information that Mr. Taylor of the Fulla Beans account was in town for one more night, and that he was prepared to reconsider his decision about withdrawing the account.

'Now you take him out to dinner,' Uncle Ralph said.

'Tell him our plans, lay it on thick. Get him drunk, entertain him. Take him to a night-club and fix him up with a hostess. Keep him happy, whatever happens, I want that account back.'

'Yes, sir.' David got up.

Penny was sitting behind her desk in the outer office, legs crossed neatly beneath her desk. She smiled at him, an open invitation in her innocent wide eyes. He wondered vaguely if she was sleeping with the old buzzard, the rumour around the building said she was. He wouldn't mind knocking a piece of that off, get one over on Uncle Ralph. He leant over her desk. 'How come I only ever see you here?'

Her smile widened and she started to reply, but the buzzer rang on her desk and she jumped up quickly. Uncle Ralph had anticipated the pass and was summoning her to the safety of his office!

She scampered off, sexy legs beneath a short skirt.

David returned morosely to his own office, and his own secretary who was pale, mousy, and flat chested and who wore long skirts. She had a mad crush on him which she tried to conceal, making it all the more obvious.

'Oh, Mr. Cooper,' she said, 'is everything all right?'

'Everything's fine,' he sat glumly at his desk, the thought of entertaining Mr. Taylor of Fulla Beans to a gay evening out on the town was depressing.

'Oh dear, Mr. Cooper,' his secretary was almost wringing her hands, 'Oh dear, it had to happen today too.'

'What's so special about today?'

'It's your divorce today.' She lowered her eyes. 'Well, I mean –'

So it was – he had forgotten all about it. It seemed strange that Linda could go into a court somewhere and divorce him and he didn't have to be there. It didn't seem right somehow.

His solicitor had written informing him of the date some time ago, and stated that they would send someone along purely as a formality.

His secretary stood nervously by his desk. 'Thanks for the cheerful reminder, Miss Field,' he said.

She flushed. 'Oh, I'm sorry – I thought you knew . . .' Her words tailed off. 'Would you like some coffee, Mr. Cooper?'

'That would be nice, Miss Field.'

She fled gratefully and almost tearfully from his office.

'Sonovabitch!' he muttered. 'Sonovabitch!'

The entrance hallway into the courts was tall and sinister and huge. There were people scurrying in all directions, and long passages and stairs everywhere. The overall atmosphere was one of gloom.

Linda's solicitor gripped her firmly by the arm and manoeuvred her along up various flights of stairs and into a couple of old elevators. It seemed to take ages to get whereever they were going.

'I hope your case will be heard before the luncheon recess,' her solicitor said, 'chances are that it will be.'

'How long will it take?' Linda asked nervously.

'Not too long, it's all very straightforward, shouldn't take long at all.'

They had arrived in a long hallway with benches along the walls, and this, Linda presumed, was where they were going to wait. It was crowded with people and there were a scattering of men in long white curled wigs and black gowns. Her solicitor called one of them over. 'This is your counsel, Mr. Brown.'

Mr. Brown was tall and distinguished looking, with a tanned crinkly face. He had a soothing hypnotic voice, and he discussed the questions he would ask Linda briefly. She felt sick. The whole thing was so awful. Her stomach was fluttering, she wondered if there was a ladies' room close at hand where she could go and collapse.

Her solicitor was saying, 'I think it might be a good idea if we go in and sit through a couple of cases before yours. It will give you a chance to see how things are done.'

She nodded bleakly. He led her through an ordinary door into an ordinary room, and she got a jolting shock. Instead of a huge stately-looking court room as she had imagined, it was a small plain room with about six rows of benches where onlookers sat, a small slightly raised desk where the judge sat, and a raised wooden dais where the witness stood. It was awful. Everyone was so close to everyone else. It was like someone's living-room converted into a court for a day.

She sat on a bench in horror. A lightly built man was standing on the witness dais being questioned.

'And did you know at that time that your wife had had intercourse with Mr. Jackson?'

'Yes, sir.'

'And it was the same day that she packed her bags and left?'

'Yes, sir.'

'Leaving you in the matrimonial home with the children of your marriage, Jennifer and Susan?'

'Yes, sir.'

The case droned on. The slightly built man expressionless as he was asked question after question.

The judge sat wisely on his bench, nodding occasionally and looking for all the world like a senile old owl. At the conclusion of evidence he said, in hardly more than a mumble, 'Divorce granted. Custody of the children. Maintenance referred to chambers. Next case, please.'

The expressionless slight man suddenly broke into smiles, his shoulders straightened and he left the room happily.

The next case was a mousy-looking blonde with a heavy Cockney accent who was out to divorce Joe – from the sound of it, a wildly attractive sex maniac. It's so unfair, Linda thought, we're the innocent ones, and we're the ones who have got to stand up in this stupid little room and reveal the most personal aspects of our lives.

'Were your marital relationships satisfactory at first?' Counsel asked.

'I should say so!' Mousey blonde replied, drawing a muffled ribald laugh from somewhere in the courtroom.

At last it was Linda's turn. She stood shakily in the witness stand, horribly aware of how close everyone was to her. She resented the rows of spectators, why should they be allowed to sit there and stare and listen. It wasn't fair. After she was sworn in her counsel began the questions. She answered in a muffled quiet voice, eyes staring straight ahead. A document was produced from an equity agent and the judge inspected it briefly. Her counsel continued with the questions which were really statements of fact which she had only to confirm. Eventually he indicated to the judge that he was finished.

The judge adjusted his glasses, peered for a few brief seconds at Linda, and then said, 'Divorce granted, custody of the two children and costs to be paid by the husband. Maintenance and access referred to chambers.'

It was all over. She left the stand in a daze. Her solicitor

97

came and took her arm. 'Congratulations,' he whispered.

Giles was late of course, he was always late. He was strung with cameras and looked tired. 'Give me some strong black coffee, darling,' he said. 'I've had a terrible morning shooting bras in the middle of the New Forest.'

He collapsed in a chair, stretching his legs out and yawning. 'Y'know this is a great pad, almost worth putting up with your boy-friend.'

'Almost?' questioned Claudia. She had done a skilful make-up, pale creamy matt base, clever blended rouge, pale brown lipstick and huge flattery eyes. She looked fabulous.

'Yeah, almost. I mean, darling he's such a square. Hey, you look divine, wish we were shooting this at night, how late can I stay?'

'Well, until my lord and master gets home, I guess – you know how jealous he is. I'll give him a buzz around five and see what time he'll be home.'

'I want to shoot some wild stuff on the terrace – sort of get you silhouetted against the view of London jazz. Lots of hair flowing about and all that gear.'

'Sounds cool.' She was wearing a pink denim shirt tucked into matching hipster pants with a huge gold buckled belt and white boots.

'Great outfit,' he said, 'we can start off with that, discarding it bit by bit.'

'So how's your love life?' she asked. 'Still with that skinny model?'

'Yeah, we break up about every two weeks regularly, but then it's back together again time.'

'I see her on the cover of every magazine I pick up, it's amazing, 'cos I mean she's not really that great-looking, but she photographs beautifully.'

'Well, she's got a camera face, y'know. She sees a camera and the face switches on, comes to life, otherwise it's just static! I guess our affaire keeps going because she's really screwing my camera and I love the results. She's making me a bomb. I can't miss with anything I shoot of her.'

The 'phone rang. It was Claudia's agent, excited and pleased. It was true, the unit was returning at the end of the week and Claudia would probably be needed the following week.

'The director is flying in today,' her agent said, 'and the

company is going to try and pin him down to a definite date.'

'Oh, fabulous.' Claudia was delighted, she had waited six months for this.

'Let's get started, darling,' Giles said when she hung up, 'before I go to sleep.'

Giles worked fast, using three different cameras. He threw himself completely into it, becoming utterly absorbed in what he was doing. Claudia of course blossomed before a camera, pouting, smiling, giving a tiger snarl, big, big sexy eyes always innocently staring, lips open and glossy. She undid the pink shirt, letting it fall casually open. There was nothing underneath.

After a while Giles said, 'Take your shirt off and fold your arms across your boobies. That's it – great! Give me a snarl. That's beautiful, baby. One leg slightly bent – a surprised look, marvellous! Now cover your boobies with your hands, give me the big-eyed baby look – beautiful!'

Giles kept shooting picture after picture. 'You look divine, darling, turn your back to me and swing your head around quickly let your hair fall – great! Hey listen, I've got a terrific idea if you don't mind getting wet. Put the shirt back on and I'll hose you down with water, it will look very effective.' He picked up the water hose used to water the plants, and turned it on her. She screamed and giggled, 'It's cold!' He dropped the hose and picked up his camera.

He was right, it was effective. Her clothes had moulded themselves to her body, and her nipples stood out firm and strong through the shirt.

After an hour on the terrace Giles said, 'Crazy, let's go inside, baby. I've got some beautiful stuff of you out here.'

She was shivering. 'Lead the way to the shower,' he said, 'I don't want you catching cold. Strip off slowly, I want to capture it all.'

He followed her into the bathroom with his cameras, watching every moment as she wriggled out of her wet clothes and secured her hair with a couple of pins. As she stood under the shower, her body gleamed as the rivulets of water hit her, he said, 'Lean back, close your eyes, just let the water fall over you. Great! Bring you arms up behind your head, lovely, darling, that's lovely.'

They finished in the bathroom and Giles said, 'Now for some jazz in the bedroom and then we should have it made.'

She put on a filmy black chiffon robe, trimmed with feathers, and let her hair down. The robe was transparent, casting a black haze over her body.

'Lie right in the middle of the bed, bring your head up, bend one knee ever so slightly, no, your left knee, darling – that's it. Wet your lips and give me the look. No, that's too hard, a soft look like you just made it.'

He took a few shots and then put his camera down. 'Listen, you want these pictures to look really good?'

'Of course I do – what's the matter?' She sat up, her perfect breasts falling free of the robe.

'Darling, you just haven't got the right look, you're trying too hard, more relaxed, please.'

She stretched. 'I'm relaxed.'

'Yeah, I know, but you know what I want, I want the cat that just got the cream look.'

'So give me the cream . . .' she reached for him.

'Just what I had in mind.'

They made love easily, slowly, almost offhandedly, and afterwards he got quickly up, and picked up his camera. 'Stay just as you are. That's perfect. *Now* you look authentic!'

David 'phoned Claudia at five o'clock. He had been trying to make up his mind whether to take her along with Mr. Taylor of Fulla Beans or not. Eventually he decided it would be better not to take her, as he would pay more attention to her than to Mr. Taylor, and that would defeat the purpose of the whole outing.

'What are you doing, darling?' he asked. She giggled, 'Oh, just lying around.'

He put her in the picture about the evening ahead and she said, 'That's all right, I'll find something to do.'

'Why don't you get an early night and I'll wake you when I get in?'

She suddenly laughed. 'Hey, David, I feel like a wife. Are you sure you haven't got some dolly little bird standing by your side?'

'Honestly, Claudia, don't be so stupid.'

'Well, baby, don't worry about it, I don't mind, anything you can do I can do too.'

'Listen, it's a business dinner. Now what are you going to do?'

She paused, then said, 'The President of America.'

'What?'

She laughed. 'I'm only joking! Go on, I believe you. Have a nice dinner, I shall probably ask a few people over, and we'll sit around and wait for your esteemed return.'

'All right,' he said reluctantly, 'an early night would do you much more good.'

'You're beginning to sound so stuffy,' she mimicked his voice, 'an early night would do you much more good!'

He ignored her comment. 'I'll 'phone you later. Be good.'

'Yes, sir, anything else, sir?'

'Goodbye.' He put the 'phone down, annoyed at the way she spoke to him. Annoyed by the fact that he was still so jealous of her. Annoyed by the fact she was going to ask people over. He would have to try and find Mr. Taylor a randy hostess and get rid of him early. He went into his private bathroom to change his shirt and shave.

Miss Field knocked nervously to say goodnight, and he rewarded her with a glimpse of his naked chest. She blushed deeply and he wondered idly if she had ever been laid. He really couldn't imagine it. She wore long knee length pink bloomers which he had noticed when she sat opposite him taking dictation. Also she was flat-chested, and who would want to lay a flat-chested ugly girl? Once he had screwed the most horrifying-looking girl, cross-eyed, bad teeth, acne, but she had had the best and biggest knockers he'd ever seen and wild legs. She had been a great lay too, but he hadn't bothered to see her again, that face was too much.

David had met Mr. Taylor once before briefly. He was middle-aged and running to fat, he had thinning brown hair plastered neatly to his scalp to give the impression that it wasn't thinning at all, but just grew that way. He had a thick Lancashire accent and thick Lancashire wife with two matching sons. He was a bore.

David met him in the bar of his hotel. He had been drinking lager beer but switched to scotch as soon as David arrived. David tried to be charming – but Burt Taylor's idea of charming was a person who drank fast and told an everlasting run of dirty stories. David tried to please, and Burt rewarded him with hearty guffaws and conspiratorial winks. By the time they arrived at the restaurant David was well on the way and Burt already there – drunk, that is.

David tried to insert a little business into the conversation, but Burt switched it neatly back to the subject of sex by remarking how he bet David had a lot of hot ones passing through his job.

'All those little model girls,' Burt said, 'that's how they get the job, by sleeping with you, isn't it?' David didn't argue.

Eventually they reeled out of the restaurant arm in arm, Burt singing snatches of old Rugby songs. David patted Burt on the back. 'Let's go and have some fun then.'

They went to a plushy night-club, filled with tired painted hostesses and jocular lecherous out of town businessmen on expense accounts. The Maitr'de, a smooth suave Cypriot, asked if they would care to meet two nice young ladies.

'Oh yes,' Burt boomed, 'only make sure they're not all that nice.' He roared with laughter.

A few minutes later two girls arrived at their table, one was tall and buxom, with red hair and a strapless green velvet dress, she was about thirty. The other was smaller and slightly timid-looking – in spite of a dress cut low enough to reveal almost all of her scrawny bosom. She was very young. They both tried to attach themselves to David, but he excused himself from the table, realizing he hadn't phoned Claudia. He tried to sound sober, but there was so much noise and music on the other end of the 'phone that it was difficult to hear anything. A man answered the 'phone and he was told to hang on while the mystery voice located Claudia.

David hung grimly on to the 'phone, feeling the alcohol pounded out of his body by a sudden mad anger. By the time she reached the 'phone he felt almost sober.

'Hi, darling,' she cooed, 'where are you? I'm having a marvellous time, it turned into a party.'

'Who answered the 'phone? Who's there?'

'Oh, I don't know, heaps of people. Hurry home, baby.' And she hung up.

He stood in the phone booth for a few minutes, then intent on getting rid of Burt Taylor, he hurried back to the table. Burt had ordered champagne naturally, since David would be paying the bill. The two hostesses were flanking him on either side and he looked blissfully happy.

David thought the best thing to do was to get hold of the big brassy redhead and proposition her to take Mr. Burt Taylor off somewhere, he obviously preferred her to the younger one.

There was a cheesy Latin American band playing. 'How about a dance?' he said directly to the redhead. She smelt heavily of cheap perfume, and pressed herself groin to groin with him.

He managed to push her away a little and said, 'Hey listen, you want to make yourself a few pounds?'

She looked interested. David explained the proposition. They bargained, reached an agreement, and sat down, David carefully slipping her the money beforehand.

Burt Taylor was a bit put out. He took him to one side and said, 'I saw her first, boyo, I don't want the skinny bit.'

David smiled, this was going to be easy. 'It's all right, she can't stop talking about you, you've got it made.'

'Well, in that case . . .' Burt leered, 'we won't be wasting too much more time here.'

David reckoned another half-an-hour and he would be home. He patted Burt on the shoulder – 'I'll get the bill,' he said.

There were photographers outside the court waiting for Linda. The fact that Claudia Parker had been named as the other woman made the case almost newsworthy.

'Over here,' one of them called. Linda rushed ahead, her solicitor gripping her arm. The cameras clicked.

'What do they want?' she questioned. 'Can't they leave people alone. I'm nobody.'

Her solicitor hailed a passing taxi and pushed her in. 'It's best for you to get away from here. Congratulations again, we'll be in touch with you.'

'Can't I give you a lift?' she asked, trying to delay being left on her own.

'No, no, my office is just round the corner. Goodbye, Mrs. Cooper.' He was gone and the taxi was moving off down the street.

'Where to, lady?' asked the cab driver. She sat there slightly dazed, it had all happened so quickly, it was like a dream. 'Where to, lady?' the cab driver repeated, slightly impatient.

She didn't feel like rushing straight to the station, she felt like a drink and a cigarette and a half hour of quiet relaxation. 'The Dorchester,' she said.

The bar was fairly crowded, mostly with businessmen, but she found a secluded table, ordered a sherry and sat back to enjoy it. She decided she would have lunch there. It was good to be on her own. She would order smoked salmon and boeuf strogonoff, fresh strawberries with cream maybe even drink champagne.

'It is Linda Cooper, isn't it?' She looked up, hesitated and then said, 'Jay – Jay Grossman. Why I would hardly have recognized you, what a wonderful tan.'

He sat down, smiling. 'I just got in from Israel. How are you? It's been months and months.'

'I'm fine,' she smiled back at him.

'And David?'

'David? I don't really know. I just divorced him about half-an-hour ago.'

Jay looked surprised. 'You really did it then. Was it about that night?'

She nodded. 'Yes, it was about that night. He's living with her now.'

'Wow, you certainly mean what you say.'

'How is Lori?'

'Lori is very happy. Lori is married to a Texas oil tycoon who buys her two mink coats a week, so she's very happy.'

'You mean you've divorced too?'

'Yes, I'm divorced yet again, we do these things quickly in the States. She went to Nevada and shed me in six weeks on extreme mental cruelty – then married this other man the very next day. The only good thing is she didn't knock me for any alimony or settlements so I was lucky. Supporting the other two ex's costs me enough.' He laughed. 'Are you meeting anyone?'

She shook her head.

'Well, what about having lunch with me?'

She smiled, she liked Jay. 'I'd love to.'

'Good.' He stood up. 'I've just got to rearrange a few things, I'll be right back.'

After he left Linda quickly took out her compact. She studied her face and added more lipstick. She wished she looked a bit more glamorous, but she had deliberately put on her dress-down clothes to appear in court. Jay was a very attractive man. Since separating from David, Linda had only been out with a man once, partly because her solicitor had warned her not to, and partly because she didn't want to. The episode with Paul had left its mark, and she preferred to stay at home or perhaps visit married friends. The evening she had gone out had been an utter bore, and to add insult to injury the man she had been with had immediately expected her to go to bed with him. Divorcees, she gathered from him, were supposed to include sex in the evening's activities.

Jay returned to the table. 'Everything under control, where would you like to eat?'

They decided to stay where they were. They moved into the restaurant, and Jay entertained her with amusing anecdotes about the location and idle gossip about the people involved.

He took her hand over coffee and said, 'My God, it's nice to be with someone who has a brain and not just a body. You know, I really like you Linda, you're a really nice person.' She smiled a little stiffly, she didn't want Jay to think of her as such a nice person. Nice was such a dull word, it conjured up twinsets and sensible shoes.

He looked at his watch. 'Wow – it's nearly three o'clock, I've got to rush.' He called for the bill. 'Let me drop you at the station. I've got a studio car.'

'No, it's right out of your way, I can easily get a cab.'

'Oh, O.K., if you insist. I'll put you in the cab though.'

They left the restaurant and walked through the lobby where Jay was hailed by a couple standing there. The woman was tall, blonde and pretty, the man short, stocky and red-faced. The man said, 'Oh, Mr. Grossman, sorry you couldn't make lunch. This is my client, Miss Susan Standish.'

Miss Susan Standish smiled a direct smile at Jay, she had very small white teeth and she looked even prettier when she smiled. Jay smiled back. Linda saw his eyes flicker with interest as they swept over Miss Standish. Tall pretty blondes were obviously his type.

'I'll be right back,' he said, and took Linda to the entrance. He made no comment about the couple he had obviously stood up for lunch. He kissed her on the cheek, 'Linda, let's do this again sometime. When will you be back?'

'Thank you for a lovely lunch, Jay. I'll be back Monday.'

He saw her into a cab. 'I'll talk to you then,' he said.

The phone rang and Claudia stretched languorously across the bed and picked it up. She spoke briefly, and with a grin she hung up.

'Baby,' she said to Giles, 'tonight we can swing, Daddy won't be home till late!'

Giles said, 'What are we waiting for, let's have a party, get on the 'phone. Call the liquor store first.'

They picked out names at random. Giles would say, 'Remember that kooky little girl who always wore those terrible thigh length black boots . . .' and they would track her down, inviting another half a dozen people en route. Claudia changed into a startling silver lamé cat suit. Giles snatched a nap, sprawled across her bed, and eventually people began to appear.

By the time David 'phoned again the party was in full swing. Claudia was completely stoned. She didn't even know half the people who were there. The music was so loud that the tenants in the flat below had complained three times. They had stopped 'phoning as the last time a beautifully spoken debutante had told them exactly what to do in explicit detail. She was now accommodating an out-of-work window cleaner on the sofa in full view of everyone.

'Swinging party!' Giles said. 'What happens when big daddy comes walking in?'

'Big daddy's going to have to join in the fun or big daddy can walk right out again.'

'Darling, sweetie-pie – how divine of you to invite me.'

Claudia blinked, focusing slowly. 'Shirley baby, how are you?'

'I'm fine, simply fine. Just got back from the most divine holiday.'

'You look great, just great – all that crazy suntan. Where's the Hon. what not?'

'Ditched him, darling. I've got the most divine man now, simply a poppet. You'll be amazed.'

'Grab a drink, darling, and join in, it's all happening here . . .'

Claudia trailed off as a Spanish-looking gentleman grabbed her from behind – 'You is beautiful,' he said, 'I eat you up.'

'Really,' Shirley said, 'it looks like you're in good hands, I'll see you later, sweetie.'

She left Claudia struggling with the boy. Claudia had never seen him before. 'Leave me alone, you oaf,' she said. He was very strong. 'You beautiful,' he said proudly, obviously his English vocabulary was limited. He twisted her round in his arms and kissed her. 'Your breath stinks!' she exclaimed, still struggling. He held her even tighter and kissed her again. It was at this moment that David appeared. He stood, shocked, in the doorway of the apartment. He spotted Claudia immediately, and striding across the room he hauled the Spanish boy away from her – smashing his fist into his face. The boy slumped to the floor, blood seeping from his nose.

'You little tramp,' he said, and brought his arm backhandedly across her face.

Nobody really noticed what was going on, the music was too loud and they were all too stoned.

'Get these dregs out of here,' David snarled at her. She rubbed her cheek, her eyes huge and filled with tears – more from pain than from anything else. 'You lousy sonofabitch,' she muttered, 'how dare you hit me – how dare you.'

'I'll do what I want to, I bought you, didn't I? Now get this damned place clear.'

'You can go to hell,' she ran over to the Spanish boy and cradled his head in her arms.

'I'm warning you, Claudia, you're pushing me too far.'

She continued to cradle the boy's head and ignored him.

He stood for a few seconds, then said, 'Right.' He marched off into the bedroom. It was at this particular moment that Giles was reaching a hard fought-for climax with a black girl. It was unfortunate that it happened to be right in the middle of David's bed. David swore loudly, but nothing bothered Giles, and he kept on going, although the girl squeaked and attempted to object.

David grimly took a suitcase from the top of a cupboard, he methodically sorted his clothes from Claudia's, packing as much as he could.

Giles and the girl got up. She glared at David as she rearranged her clothes. 'Some people don't care,' she muttered, 'they just barge in anywhere.'

Giles made a mock bow – 'Performance over, next show at four o'clock.'

They walked out of the bedroom.

David locked the door behind them and continued packing. He finally filled three suitcases. His mind was cold with anger. He unlocked the bedroom and strode to the front door with two of the cases – the party was still in full swing. He returned for the third suitcase.

' 'Bye 'bye darling,' Claudia screamed above the noise, she was reeling across the room towards him, the front zipper on her cat suit was undone, almost to her waist, and her breasts pushed forward to escape. Her hair was wild and blood was smeared across her face.

'You look lovely,' he said, 'just like the drunken little whore you are.'

She laughed. 'Get stuffed,' she shouted, 'get lost – don't come back, you're a bloody bore.'

Giles joined her – 'You tell him, darling,' he said, slipping his hand inside the open zipper. She made an obscene gesture and turned her back.

David left.

CHAPTER FOURTEEN

'Well, look darling, what is happening?' Claudia's voice was edgy and cold on the 'phone. 'I mean they have been back ten days now, and they should be able to tell us something.'

Her agent was non-commital. 'I can't get any definite date out of them.'

'But I signed a contract for two days' work a contract, remember?'

'Yes, I know, but they've paid you for the two days' work you were supposed to do. You got the £160 already, so they don't have to use you.'

She snorted angrily. 'What kind of an agent are you? I'm supposed to be in that film. It's a big film and it will do me a lot of good – a lot more good than these walk-on bits you keep offering me. If you can't do it, tell me – tell me and I'll get someone who can!'

Her agent's voice was resigned. 'I'm doing my best.'

'Well, your best's not enough. Forget it, I'll do it myself, I'll call Conrad Lee.' She slammed the 'phone down.

'Stupid agents! They never do a thing for you except take your money.'

The flat was in a terrible mess. The new daily had walked out the day after the party. Actually, the party had still been going on the next morning when she arrived and she had taken one horrified look at the red-headed boy wearing Claudia's cat-suit who answered the front door, and she left.

It had been a good party, lasted three days in all. Claudia didn't remember too much about it really – but Giles assured her it had been a gas.

David hadn't returned. He hadn't 'phoned and he hadn't communicated in any way, although a mousy secretary had arrived one day about a week later to collect his mail and request that in future it be forwarded to his office. Claudia didn't miss him. She was rather glad he had gone really. Life was too confining with someone watching every move you made.

Claudia was really a very independent girl. She had fallen in with David because it was easy and he had left his wife, and it just sort of happened. It was rather nice having all the bills paid and lots of new clothes and no problems. She would have to think about going back to work, a secret job she had which had always given her enough money to lead a comfortable independent life. It would be better though to be in Conrad's movie, and become a star and make lots more money that way.

The other way gave her a vicarious thrill though, and none of her friends, no one knew about it. She had always kept it a closely guarded secret and before she was living with David all her friends had wondered but never found out how she always managed to be so financially secure and independent. The job excited her, she wore wigs and did special creative make-up jobs completely disguising her own features. She starred in glorious technicolour in blue movies! In four years she had been in thirty of them, earning at least eight or nine hundred pounds per film. So successful was she at the disguise jobs that she was known as three completely different girls, all in constant demand by the voyeurs who got to see the finished product. If she wanted to work again, all it would take would be a 'phone call.

This is Evette – or Carmen – or Maria, and arrangements would be made. She was paid cash, and she contacted them

– they had no way of reaching her. It was a satisfactory arrangement.

However, she wasn't sure that she wanted to go back to doing that. Sometimes her co-stars left a lot to be desired, and of course if you weren't in the right mood, it could be pretty grim.

No – to appear in Conrad's movie would be the best thing, and if her agent couldn't fix it, she certainly would. Conrad would probably be delighted to hear from her again.

She 'phoned the hotel he had stayed at on his previous visit, but he wasn't registered there. She 'phoned the studio and spoke to a secretary who took her name and said she would pass Mr. Lee her message. She tried to find out where he was living, but the girl was polite but firm – 'we're not allowed to disclose Mr. Lee's address,' she said, 'but I'll certainly see he gets your message.' It wasn't very satisfactory, Claudia wanted to get him personally. Giles would be able to find out. Giles was working for the 'in' magazine of the moment and they seemed to be able to get hold of anyone. She called him at the studio, but there was no reply.

'Oh dammit,' she muttered, finally getting up. There was a stack of bills at the front door. David had stopped paying for everything since he had left, and the bills were steadily mounting. She couldn't stick him with any of them as the flat and everything was in her name. It was a question of getting hold of Conrad and becoming a star. 'Once I get hold of that old bald buzzard, no problem,' she laughed, 'he'll be putty in my hands.'

Linda stayed in the country with her parents and the children much longer than she expected to. It was so peaceful, the children were out playing all day and she sat in the house while her mother fussed around her. It was very relaxing, and knowing that to return to London was to be the beginning of a new life, she clung on to the limbo period of being with her parents.

Her mother wanted her to stay there permanently. 'Sell your house,' she urged Linda, 'there's plenty of room for you here.'

Linda rejected the offer. Her parents' home was just a temporary retreat, and tempting as the thought was, it would be a mistake to stay. She would be buried there, stifled. Her mother would take care of everything, even to

110

bringing up the children. Linda would become the elder daughter of the family.

One Saturday afternoon David turned up. It was the first time she had seen him since they separated.

'I tried 'phoning the house, I was worried,' he said. 'I thought you'd be here.'

Her voice was stilted, cold. 'Why didn't you 'phone here? Why did you just come?'

He was ill at ease, it was strange to see David groping for words – he who was usually so sure of himself. 'I wanted to see the children,' a note of indignation crept into his voice, almost a whine, she thought. 'I'm supposed to see the children, you know.'

He looked thin and tired. 'I've left Claudia,' he blurted out.

She looked at him dispassionately. 'Oh!'

'You look marvellous,' he said.

She did look well. Her skin was glowing from long walks in the country and her hair was shining and unset, tied casually back with a ribbon, and she looked very slim in a pair of slacks and a loose shirt.

'Well,' she shrugged, 'the children are in the garden, I'll call them in.'

He put a hand on her arm. 'I said I've left Claudia.'

She brushed his hand impatiently away. 'I heard you the first time, David. I'll get the children.' She walked quickly from the room.

He stayed the whole afternoon, chatting amicably to her parents, entertaining Jane and Stephen with all sorts of games. David is turning on his well known charm, Linda thought miserably, I wish he'd go away.

He finally left at six. Her mother wanted to ask him to stay to dinner – but Linda hissed at her – 'Don't you dare.' His charm had worked. 'He really wants you back,' her mother said after he had gone. She was really saying you should go back to him. Linda knew the signs. Her father was less direct.

'The boy needs a father,' he said, when Stephen played up before going to bed. Her mother said later in the evening, 'Poor David looks so unhappy.'

It was too much for Linda, they just didn't understand. They meant well, but she had had enough.

The next morning she told them she was going back to

London, and on Monday morning, she packed, and amidst tears from her mother, and gruff words of wisdom from her father, she and the children were put safely on a train.

She was glad to be back in her own house. The children were pleased and excited to be reunited with all their books and toys, and cries of 'super' and 'that's mine' rang through the house.

Anna gave her a list of 'phone messages, and amongst them were two calls from Jay Grossman. He had left his number. She didn't call back, she wanted to, but somehow she felt if he really wanted to see her again he would try once more to 'phone.

Monica had 'phoned her. They hadn't spoken since the separation, they were David's friends. She 'phoned Monica who was delighted. 'Dahling,' she exclaimed, 'I'm having a little dinner party – I'd love you to come.'

Linda was hesitant. 'When?'

'Tomorrow night, sweetie, I must see you, it's been such ages. Will you come?'

'I don't know, Monica. I mean, have you invited David?'

'Dahling! What do you take me for? Of course not. I don't want any other excuses. I'll see you tomorrow, eight o'clock. Don't be late.'

That was settled then. It might be fun, Monica always invited interesting people. She would go the hairdresser's, and then buy a new dress. It was about time she started going out again.

Claudia sprawled untidily on the sofa at the back of Giles' studio. He was hard at work photographing a languid brunnette clad only in a silver bodystocking.

Claudia yawned. 'Why the hell don't you answer your bloody 'phone, you could have saved me a trip.'

Giles didn't look round, his concentration was completely on the model. After a few minutes he stopped, told the girl to take a break and wandered over to Claudia, lighting a cigarette. He stuck it in her mouth and she took a long drag. She spluttered and choked – 'Jesus Christ! Smoking pot at this time of day! You're too much!'

He laughed, took back his cigarette and said, 'What the hell do you want?'

'I came to see you,' she replied coyly.

'Cut the crap, I'm busy. What do you want?'

'Well, actually,' she stretched, 'I need Conrad Lee's number – I thought if you called your magazine they would have it.'

'Things must be tough if you're creeping back on that bandwagon.'

Her voice was irritable, sometimes she couldn't stand Giles. 'Things are not tough – and I'm not climbing back on any bandwagon.'

He laughed – 'Don't forget it's me you're talking to, baby.'

'How could I possibly forget?'

They exchanged stares. 'All right,' he said, 'keep cool, I'll get it for you.' He 'phoned the magazine and they gave him the number. Claudia wrote it down and smiled. 'Thank you, darling,' she purred.

'That's all right sweetheart – now get the hell out of here, I've got work to do.'

Claudia went shopping. She bought a white and gold silk jersey dress, and gold spikey-heeled shoes, unfashionable but sexy. She went to the hairdresser's and had her hair elaborately piled on top of her head. Back home, she bathed, splashing half a bottle of musky oil into the bath. She took two hours with her make-up – making sure it was perfect. By the time she dressed it was seven o'clock. She dialled the number Giles had given her. Conrad's unmistakably accented voice answered.

She smiled, it was all going to work perfectly. Her voice was cool and efficient.

'Mr. Lee?'

'Yes.' His voice was gruff.

'I am calling for *Star* magazine, as you know we are featuring your photograph on our cover this week, and I wondered if you might answer a few short questions about yourself.'

His voice was now friendly – 'My picture huh? Sure I'll answer a few questions.'

Conceited pig! 'Oh thank you, Mr. Lee, if you will just give me your address I'll be right over, and it will only take a few minutes.'

He was surprised, 'Can't I answer them now?'

'Oh no, Mr. Lee, it's important to get the personal reactions.'

113

'All right, all right.' He gave her his address, and, nearly laughing, she put down the 'phone.

She admired her reflection in the mirror one last time and buzzed the doorman for a cab.

Conrad lived in an imposing house in Belgravia. The door bell was answered by a manservant in a white jacket and he ushered her into the library. She waited patiently for fifteen minutes until at last Conrad lumbered in. He hadn't changed. A fat cigar stuck from between his fleshy lips, and he was wearing the same green silk smoking jacket.

She arose, deliberately posing her body so that the thin silk dress clung even tighter. She knew she had never looked better. 'Hi,' she smiled provocatively.

He came to an abrupt standstill. She could see he didn't recognize her. He plucked the cigar from his mouth – 'Are you the broad from *Star*?'

'Do I look like a lady journalist?'

His piercing eyes roved over her body. His memory stirred. 'Hey – you're the broad from the party I gave.' His voice changed. 'Hey – what's going on here – what is this?'

'You're a difficult man to get hold of. I've left lots of messages for you.'

'So?'

'I thought it was about time we got together again. Don't tell me you've forgotten all the fun we had together last time.'

Interest flickered briefly in his eyes.

'Listen, I've got guests, you stay here and I'll see what I can do.'

He left the room and she smiled triumphantly. It was amazing what a fabulous body could do.

He was gone a long time and the manservant came in with a drink and left her some magazines. She leafed idly through them waiting, because eventually he would be back and then tomorrow morning, enter Claudia Star!

CHAPTER FIFTEEN

From the day he walked out on Claudia, David felt depressed. It wasn't that he had wanted to stay, the whole situation had become impossible. Claudia was a slut, an out and out slut. She lolled around reading stupid magazines all day, only bothering with her appearance if they were going out. Staying in bed until noon or later, never tidying the flat. The only thing she seemed capable of was incessant love-making, and whereas before he had lived with her he had always been ready, now he was tired. She was insatiable – demanding, demanding and never getting enough. David had always prided himself on his sexual appetite, but this was ridiculous.

He was pleased to have an excuse to get out. He was depressed because instead of dismissing the whole Claudia mess from his mind and going home to his wife and children, he was an outcast, he had nowhere to go except to the coldness of a hotel room. There is nothing quite so bleak as living in a hotel. No privacy, no warmth, just four impersonal walls, a cold bathroom, and a Do Not Disturb sign.

He returned to work with a vengeance, and sat and brooded on the possibilities of getting back together with Linda.

He reasoned that she should take him back, after all there were the children to consider, they would want him back. A divorce could easily be rescinded, and everything could be like it was before, only this time he wouldn't be such a fool and get hooked up with a slut like Claudia. He would be more careful, pick and choose, short casual affaires, nothing that Linda could discover. He 'phoned his ex-home and the maid informed him that Linda and the children were in the country with her parents. He was pleased. Give Linda a little more time to get over it. She was a sensible woman, she would know it was right for them to be together. The first Saturday he was free he drove down to see her.

Linda looked surprisingly fresh and well. She was cold towards him, it was only to be expected. He told her about leaving Claudia, her reaction was strangely negative. Oh well, give her time.

He was charming to her parents, he knew they were on his side.

Later he drove back to London and called an old girlfriend, she was giggly and a bit stupid. They went to a movie and then back to her place. She was lousy in bed. She had none of the franticness of Claudia or the calmness of Linda. He left after an hour.

He woke early on Sunday, he had nothing to do. On an impulse he decided to go to his office and work. He had a backlog of letters and all sorts of odd things to sort out that he never had time for during the week. He wished his secretary was available, maybe she was, she looked the sort of mini-ann person who would never make plans. Poor plain Miss Field. He telephoned her.

Her voice was timid, 'Chesterfield 4521.'

'Miss Field, Mr. Cooper here.'

'Oh!' her voice became a startled squeak as if she had been caught doing something she shouldn't have been.

'Miss Field, how do you feel about working today?'

'Oh Mr. Cooper – oh, really?'

'It's quite all right if you've already made other plans.'

'Oh no – oh no – Oh, Mr. Cooper, of course I can work today.'

'Good, I'll see you down at the office in about an hour.'

She was there before him, waiting like a pale white mouse outside the locked main door.

'You look very nice today, Miss Field,' he said.

She had brushed her thin stringy brown hair down instead of scragged back and she wore a harsh scarlet lipstick on her thin usually colourless mouth. Sunday clothes consisted of an off-white dress and blue woollen cardigan. She was a picture of plainness.

They worked efficiently through the day non-stop, until the light began to fade and David suddenly realized it was getting late.

'I suppose we should call it a day,' he said, yawning. 'You must be hungry.'

'Mr. Cooper,' her voice was hesitant, nervous, 'perhaps you would care to have a little dinner with me.' A bright red flush was spreading up into her hairline. 'I make it my business to always prepare a Cordon Bleu dinner on Sundays – one of my little hobbies and I would be only too delighted if you would sample it.' She added quickly, 'Boeuf Stroganoff, with fresh green salad, followed by a lemon meringue pie.'

It sounded good, he had nowhere else to go. She kept blushing and he felt sorry for her. 'What a lovely idea, Miss Field. I'd be glad to.'

She lived in a tiny two-roomed flat. The sofa neatly festooned with crochet cushions, obviously did double duty as the bed.

She produced a half bottle of sherry – too sweet, and he sat and watched television while she pottered about in the kitchen.

He felt so sorry for her, poor lonely little spinster.

She prepared a delicious dinner and they drank a cheap Spanish wine. 'I brought it back from my holiday last year,' she said proudly.

After dinner she was obviously a little merry. 'I don't usually drink,' she said with a giggle. He was also slightly high having drunk half of the wine and most of the sherry before dinner. His attention was riveted on the television screen. The Beauty Maid commercial was on and there was Claudia in her bath. Familiar sharp pull in his groin.

'Oh, Mr. Cooper, our commercial.' Miss Field sat quickly down beside him on the sofa. He felt the nearness of a leg beside him – he rested his hand on her thigh, Miss Field shrieked and before he knew it her arms were around his neck and she was pulling his mouth towards the thin red line. They kissed and as Claudia vanished from the screen so his desire vanished with her. But it was too late. Miss Field was already in action. All in the space of seconds she leaped up, turned the light off, wriggled out of her cardigan and was back beside him. 'My dearest, I am yours,' she said. 'I have waited for this moment too long.'

He couldn't believe it, the whole thing was so ludicrous.

She lay back expectantly, quivering.

What should he do? She was a good secretary, he didn't want to lose her. He didn't want to hurt her feelings.

She was getting impatient. 'David, my dearest, come to me. I am not afraid.'

Oh well, he took a deep breath and ran his hands tentatively across her bosom. There was no bosom!

117

Coyly she said, 'I know I am not well endowed, but there is fire in my loins.'

Oh, my God! he thought.

Tired of waiting she locked her hands behind his head and pulled his mouth down on hers.

This is a bloody nightmare, he thought, but as her tongue worked on his mouth his body started to respond and soon he was ready again. She was angular and bony and surprisingly strong. She managed to get his trousers and pants off as he lay on top of her, then her mouth was travelling down his body and she was kissing him, and suddenly it was all over for him in a huge shaking furious bout of passion. He screamed but she didn't stop, sending him into a frenzy. A shudder enveloped her and at last she stopped, lying very still.

They lay in silence – his body sprawled across her at an angle. He could hardly believe what had just taken place. Placid, timid Miss Field Mouse certainly knew what she was doing.

He went and locked himself in the bathroom. His body was covered in red weals where her fingers had dug into him, she was a hot bitch!

When he returned to her room her cardigan was back on, and she was primly clearing the dishes. She avoided looking at him as he stepped into his shorts and trousers.

'Would you like coffee before you go, Mr. Cooper?' she said, her voice was even, only a slight flush across her cheeks indicating what had just taken place.

'Er, no thank you, Miss Field,' he took his cue from her. 'I really must get off.'

'Oh well, I do hope we can do this again.'

'Yes,' he hesitated. 'Well, goodbye then. See you at the office tomorrow.'

'Goodbye, Mr. Cooper, see you tomorrow.'

Out in the street David heaved a big sigh, he would have to get rid of her. To have her working with him at the office every day would be a horrible reminder.

Next time he would get a pretty secretary – just on the chance he should ever be thrown into an experience like that again.

He thought about Linda, about soft bosoms and warm lips. He was ready to go home.

'Linda dahling!' You look positively stunning! So slim, so young! This divorce business certainly agrees with you.' Monica led Linda into the living-room. 'It's an interesting crowd tonight, no married couples, Jack and I decided that would be fun, now let me introduce you.'

There were perhaps twelve people sitting and standing around. Linda recognized Monica's brother, a dress designer, very swish. He was with a small short squat woman wearing a very unsuitable silk pyjama suit. 'That's Princess Lorenz Alvaro with Rodney,' whispered Monica, 'exciting, isn't it?'

Linda had never heard of Princess Alvaro and she didn't see what was so exciting about it as Rodney was a well known queer.

She was soon chatting quietly to a doctor, tall, craggy faced, very pleasant. Before they had finished one martini he had invited her to dinner the following evening, and she thought why not? So she accepted. He was fairly attractive and seemed most taken with her. Definitely a nice man, not a David type at all.

More people arrived and Linda found herself wedged in a corner with the doctor telling her a long involved story about a patient of his with yellow jaundice. It was rather boring. She smiled politely and wished she hadn't accepted his dinner invitation. Doctor or not, he had a bad case of bad breath.

Idly she glanced around the room, then she saw Jay and she straightened up, smoothed down her dress and touched her hair. He hadn't seen her, he was talking to Rodney and Princess Alvaro and then he was joined by the blonde girl who had been in the lobby of the hotel that day. She looked even prettier now in a crisp white trouser suit, her hair tied on top of her head with a white ribbon. He put his arm around her and she smiled up at him.

Linda pulled her eyes away, the doctor droned on.

Monica announced that a cold buffet was being served in the other room.

'I am hungry,' Linda said.

'Oh, good heavens,' said the doctor, 'I must have been boring you stiff, let's go and eat.' He took her possessively by the elbow and steered her into the other room where she bumped straight into Jay. He held two plates of food and they almost fell. 'Linda!' He sounded pleased.

'Jay,' she said, affecting the same tone.

'Where have you been?'

'Oh, in the country with the children.'

'You look terrific.'

Did I look so terrible before? she wondered. 'Thank you.'

They stood and smiled at each other, and then the doctor's grip tightened and he said, 'We'd better get in that queue before we're too late.'

'Oh, yes.' Linda's heart was beating fast.

'See you in a minute,' Jay said, he winked and imitated an English accent. 'You'd better get in the queue.'

When Jay was out of hearing distance, the doctor said, 'These American film types are all the same.'

'Oh?'

'You know – brash, vulgar, full of themselves.'

'Do you know Jay Grossman?' Linda asked crossly.

'Let's say we have a mutual friend.'

'Who?' Linda asked rudely.

'Name no names, Hear no pack drill.'

'What?' Suddenly she hated the doctor.

He smiled secretly, 'Well, as a matter of fact, it's one of his ex-wives.'

'Oh,' she tried to sound disinterested.

'A lovely woman,' the doctor continued. 'I believe she had a terrible time with him. She just remarried.'

'Is it Lori?' Linda asked coldly.

The doctor looked surprised. 'Yes, as a matter of fact, it is. She's here in London with her husband, he's very wealthy.'

'How interesting,' Linda said sarcastically. She quickly helped herself to food and rushed back into the other room, the doctor close behind her. There was nowhere to sit. Jay was with the blonde on a sofa. 'Linda,' he called. 'You can have my seat.'

'Excuse me,' she said to the doctor. Jay stood up and she sat down. The blonde glanced at her slightly annoyed.

'Susan,' Jay said, 'I want you to meet a very good friend of mine, Linda Cooper.'

'Hello,' Susan's smile was limp.

The doctor squatted on his haunches in front of Linda, eating from his crowded plate hungrily. Jay drifted away to the other side of the room. Susan suddenly got up and

120

said to Linda, 'Perhaps your friend would like to sit here.'
She moved across the room to join Jay, and the doctor
quickly sat beside Linda. She was well and truly stuck, he
obviously had no intention of leaving her side. 'Can I drive
you home later?' he asked.

'I'm sorry, I have my car with me.'

'Oh, pity,' he shook his head. 'Maybe I should follow
you to see you get home safely,' he chuckled.

Linda could have screamed, he was such a bore! She
didn't even bother to reply. She jumped up, he got up too.

'Excuse me,' she said firmly, 'I have to go to the ladies'
room.'

It was quiet upstairs in Monica's bedroom. She sat at the
dressing-table and rearranged strands of her hair. Would
Monica think her rude if she left? She didn't really care.
She looked for her stole amongst the coats on the bed. What
a waste buying the new black chiffon dress she was wearing.
She found her stole and went downstairs, and slipped out
quietly. She would call Monica tomorrow and explain that
she had a headache and had thought it better not to bother
with goodbyes. Monica would probably be insulted, not
invite her again, but so what? It was much more fun staying
at home with the children. Back home she undressed slowly,
wondering why on earth three hours previously she had
painstakingly applied such a careful make-up and looked
forward so excitedly to Monica's dreary gathering. What
had she expected? Prince Charming? Not a boring doctor
with bad breath.

She felt depressed and old. Girls like Susan set the pace
now, in their crisp trouser suits and lithe bodies. Face up to
it, Linda, she thought, you've had your best years, you gave
them to David. You've got two children, you're divorced,
you have to settle for second best now.

She was lonely at night. Once, briefly it had crossed her
mind to 'phone Paul, but commonsense had prevailed. Maybe she had made a mistake divorcing David. Maybe she
should have given him another chance, but no, she was
right, this was better than living a lie with David.

She fell into a troubled sleep.

About an hour later the ringing of the 'phone woke her
up.

'Hello,' her voice was sleepy.

'Are you trying to avoid me?'

'What?' her mind was still sleep-filled.

'I leave messages for you, you don't return my calls, you avoid me tonight and then just run off. I want dinner with you tomorrow night, no excuses.'

'Yes, Jay,' her voice was weak.

'I'll pick you up at eight, and no calls to say you can't make it. I've 'phoned three times.'

She didn't know what to say.

'All right, tomorrow at eight,' he said after a short pause, 'and wear that black dress you had on tonight, it looks great.'

The 'phone clicked dead and she clung on to it. Suddenly everything seemed bright again. Jay Grossman was certainly not second best.

Eventually Conrad returned. He had been gone an hour and a half, and Claudia bored with the magazines and at being kept waiting was a little testy. She covered her irritation with a smile.

He was drunk, he grabbed hold of her, his fleshy hands feeling her body through the thin dress. She wriggled away, this wasn't the way she had planned it.

"Aren't we going upstairs?' she asked.

His breath, a mixture of strong garlic and scotch enveloped her as he replied, 'Sure – sure. Just want a little preliminary.' He forced his hand inside the neckline of her dress, grabbing hold of her breasts with rough fingers.

'You're hurting me,' she complained, and then – 'Hey – you're tearing my dress.' She pulled away from him again, furious at the torn dress, but still smiling provocatively. 'Let's go upstairs, lover,' she cooed, 'let's have a great scene upstairs.'

'All right take your dress off first – I want to take a look at the goods I'm getting.'

It was obviously no use arguing with him, she'd fix him when she got him in the sack. She peeled off sensuous folds of white jersey. Underneath she had on only a wisp of garter belt, and pale sheer stockings, her long legs emphasized by the exceptionally high heels she was wearing.

He lunged at her, falling to his knees and grabbing her around the waist. He sunk his teeth into her stomach and bit her hard.

She screamed with pain and kicked him away – 'You son of a bitch!'

He laughed, hollow loud rumbles.

She rubbed her stomach, her eyes glinting dangerously, her mouth a tight smile. So he wanted to play games huh? Well, she knew a few of her own.

'Come on,' he lumbered to the door. She followed him. He pushed her up the stairs ahead of him, stroking her legs, trying to feel between them.

They reached the bedroom, it was very dark, she could hardly see a thing.

'Get on the bed,' he commanded.

She climbed on to a large circular bed, grimly thinking things were going to be different in the morning, when this big slob was sober.

He switched on the lights – bright glaring lights, that hit the bed at a hard angle. She noticed a huge mirror above the bed. He climbed on top of her not even bothering to remove his clothes, just unfastening his trousers.

'Open up, baby,' he said, 'let's have some action.'

He used her brutally – crushing and grinding her, and afterwards wanting it different ways, making her do it to him at every conceivable angle. She worked hard, this was something he had to remember. It was funny really, when she became famous everyone would say she was an overnight discovery. How right they would be!

At last he was finished. Her body ached from his pressures. She was bruised and worn. She lay spreadeagled on the bed, too limp to move.

He was surprisingly full of life. 'Got a little thrill for you,' he said, 'just stay where you are.' He got off the bed and pressed a switch by the door, the mirror above the bed parted and slid easily in two, leaving a huge gap in the ceiling. A ring of smiling faces peered down at her around the gaping aperture.

She sat up, horrified.

'Just a few of my friends,' Conrad said easily, 'these two way mirrors are a great gimmick for making a party go with a bang!' He guffawed. 'Pick out who you'd like next.'

A woman's face grotesquely made up and old said, 'How about me, Conrad. Can I have a turn with her. She seems to know what it's all about.'

A man's voice said, 'No, me next, let me give her a real piece!'

'Oh God!' Claudia jumped off the bed.

'What's the matter?' Conrad asked. 'Don't you want to be in my movie?'

She stared at him, every instinct warning her to get out. But to leave now, what use was that. That wouldn't get her on the silver screen.

'All right,' she said. 'All right. I'll stay, but this time you'd better mean it.'

'I mean it,' he said blandly.

CHAPTER SIXTEEN

David managed to get through the early part of the next week without trouble. Miss Field was, as usual, the perfect quiet unobtrusive secretary. Neither of them made any reference to the previous Sunday, indeed, it was as if it had never happened. David felt that maybe it had all been a horrible dream, but some ghastly sense of foreboding warned him that it was true. The sooner he was rid of Miss Field, the better. Meanwhile their relationship was exactly the same as before. He decided to wait a couple of weeks then get her transferred to another department, maybe with a rise. She wouldn't object to that.

Mr. Taylor of the Fulla Beans account was in town. David didn't relish the thought, but as usual he was elected to entertain him. Did these poor out of towners *never* get tired of the inevitable clip joint night-club, and the pathetic, blowsy hostess? It seemed not. Once more David had to fix him up, this time with a big redhead called Dora. Dora laughed a lot, and suggested that it would be a lot of fun if Burt Taylor *and* David accompanied her back to her flat. Neither of them were too impressed with the idea, Burt because he didn't want to share her, and David because he didn't want to know! She was very insistent and when Burt

Taylor, eyes bulging at the thought of the show she was offering, started to think it wasn't such a bad idea after all, David became really fed up.

He managed to finally persuade them to go off on their own. How he hated this sort of entertaining, these night-club scrubbers weren't for him. He returned to his hotel room and went to bed.

The week dragged. Wednesday afternoon he 'phoned to speak to his children. They had just got home from school and were having tea. Anna told him Mrs. Cooper was out. He was sure Linda wouldn't mind if he popped in to see them, maybe she would let him stay for dinner. It was all a question of time with Linda, eventually she would realize the only sensible thing was to take him back. He told Anna he would be right over, she mumbled something in Spanish, he could hear the children's excited squeaks in the background.

He left the office in high humour. He went to Hamleys and filled his arms with toys. He stopped at Swiss Cottage and bought flowers.

By the time he arrived at the house it was two hours later. Linda answered the door tight-lipped and furious. She stood in the doorway, 'The children are being bathed.'

'All right, I can wait.'

She didn't move. 'David, we have an agreement you visit the children at the week-end.'

'Oh. What difference does it make? Are you going to penalize me because I want to see my children?'

She stood back wearily, she didn't want to be unfair as far as the children were concerned, after all, he was their father. 'Well, come in, but please don't do this again.'

'What do you mean? Please don't visit my children again?'

'No, David, I mean please keep to the agreed visiting times.'

'You surprise me, Linda,' he shook his head, 'I never thought you would use Janey and Stephen as a weapon against me.'

Her eyes filled with tears at the injustice of what he was saying. 'But I'm not, I'm just trying to do what's best.'

He looked at her coldly. 'And you think it's best that two innocent young children should not be allowed to see their father.'

'Oh David, you're twisting what I'm saying.'

'I'm not twisting anything, I'm just repeating you.' He thrust the flowers at her. 'Take these – or perhaps you would prefer to throw them out like you would me.'

She took the flowers. 'I'll see if bathtime is finished.'

'Can I have permission to go upstairs and see them in the bath?' His voice was acid.

'Of course.'

Stephen stood at the top of the stairs, scrubbed and clean in striped pyjamas. 'Daddy.'

Linda heard the cry of joy downstairs. She glanced at her watch, it was six o'clock. Maybe she should call Jay and tell him she couldn't keep their date. She felt so confused. David's attitude towards her was so unfair, he acted as if the whole thing was her fault. He came downstairs, Janey cuddled in his arms, Stephen clinging to his hand. He fetched the packages from the car and the children yelled with excitement.

Linda shut the door of the living-room and left them all together. She went upstairs and lay down on the bed. She had thought the most painful part of divorce was over, but when you have children it's never over, there's always a small questioning voice – 'Why doesn't Daddy live here any more? When can Daddy come back? Do you love Daddy?'

She 'phoned Jay. He was out.

After an hour she went downstairs. With a forced bright smile she said, 'Come along – time for bed, school tomorrow.'

Stephen glared at her, 'Oh, Mummy!' Janey started to cry.

David said, 'How about ten more minutes?'

'Please, Mummy,' Janey begged.

'Oh, O.K. – but no longer.' Linda glanced again at her watch, it was past seven and Jay was due at eight. She didn't want him and David to meet. She wished she could contact Jay and put him off. She didn't want to but she really didn't feel like going out now.

After another twenty minutes the children were at last safely in bed, with David reading them stories. By the time he came downstairs it was a quarter to eight. His mood was cordial. 'I could do with a drink.'

She was nervous. She had a perfect right to go out on a date, but she instinctively knew David wouldn't like it.'

David poured himself a scotch. 'You know Stephen's a very bright lad, we must have a serious talk about his future.'

She pulled herself together. 'Yes, we must, but not now. I have to get changed,' her voice became defiant. 'I'm going out.'

'That's nice.' There was a silence, then David added, 'Pretty cushy life you've got.'

Linda's voice was controlled, 'I beg your pardon?'

'Well, you know, no worries, nice house, I foot all the bills and you can just gad about doing what you like.'

'I don't gad about and you know it.'

'Oh come off it, Linda. You're an attractive woman, a divorcee. Any man knows he's on to a good thing – a bit of free crumpet is always popular, you must have dozens of offers, why I bet ...'

Her face was blazing. 'Get out! Get out of here!'

He put his drink down calmly. 'What's the matter, don't try and tell me you're not getting it.'

'Please go, David, please go right now.'

He sauntered to the door. 'All right, all right, don't get excited. I won't hang around to mess up your date, I'll just get back to my hotel room – don't worry about me, just have a good time.'

He was at the front door and she slammed it in his face.

David climbed into his car. Thoughtless bitch! She was as bad as Claudia, they were all the same, all bitches trying to grab you by the balls and squeeze everything out of you. He drove around the block and then came back and parked a few houses away. May as well wait and see who she was going out with.

Jay was a few minutes late, but hardly late enough for Linda to have time to recover. He found her in tears.

'I can't go out,' she sobbed.

He put his arm around her and she leaned her head against his chest. She told him a jumbled account of what had happened. He was sympathetic. 'You talk to your lawyer first thing tomorrow. You can get a court order to stop him bothering you – he has set times to see the kids, and he'll just have to stick to them.'

'I just thought it would be so mean of me not to let him see the children.'

'That's how he wants you to feel. He's probably had enough screwing around and wants to come back. His only way of getting at you is through the kids.'

'Do you think so?'

'Sure, listen, Linda – I'm experienced in these things. He blew a beautiful set-up with you, you're not some little ding-a-ling, you're a lovely woman, and I bet he wants you back.' He paused and then asked casually, 'How do you feel about him?'

'I don't know. I mean I don't love him or anything like that. It's just that in spite of his insults I feel sorry for him, after all, I do have the home and children and what does he have?'

'Hey, whoa baby, you're starting to think like he wants you to think. He chose, didn't he?'

She nodded. 'You're right.'

'Good, at least you're starting to realize I'm always right!' He laughed. 'Now go upstairs, powder your nose, put on your black dress and let's go.'

She smiled. 'Yes, Jay.'

He took her to Annabels. They dined elegantly. Jay entranced her with amusing stories about the film and the location in Israel. He told her about his children, there were three of them, one by his first wife and two by his second.

'Beautiful blond Californians,' he said wryly. 'I don't get to see them too much, Lori hated children.'

'How old are they?'

'Well, Caroline's the eldest, she's fifteen – a real cukoo kid. Lives in San Francisco with Jenny, my first wife. Then there's Lee, he's ten, and Lance who's nine. They've got a great stepfather now, and I see them whenever I'm in L.A.'

'I've never been to America. Is it as glossy as it all looks on the screen?'

Jay laughed, 'I guess you could say Hollywood is pretty glossy – personally he only thing I really dig there is the weather.'

After dinner they were joined by friends of Jay's, also in the movie business.

It was a lovely evening. Jay took Linda home in his chauffered studio car, he kissed her on the cheek.

'How about Saturday?' he asked.

'Yes,' she replied quietly.

'I'll call you tomorrow anyway. And don't forget, get on to your lawyer first thing.'

'I will.'

They smiled at each other. She let herself into the house and watched him through the window as he climbed back into the car. She liked him a lot.

Claudia buried herself into bed at her apartment. She huddled beneath the covers, bruised, used and frightened to face herself. She called her agent the day after the debacle with Conrad and told him everything was fixed, he should hear from the studio in about a week. She took a variety of pills and slept, or tried to.

Claudia was not naïve, there had been many men, many different scenes, the blue movies, but never anything so degrading as the evening at Conrad's house. When she closed her eyes visions of evil smiling faces swept before her, all the things they had made her do raced through her thoughts. She could still feel their hands, her body screamed from the aches of sexual misuse. She stayed underneath the covers, not eating, ignoring the telephone, inert and numb for several days. Nobody cared, nobody came. If she died it would probably be months before they discovered her. Where were all her so-called friends? At last she forced herself to get up. She was thin and white. She dressed and went out. The people in the street disgusted her. She went to see Giles, he was away in Majorca. She returned home and hacked off all her tawny glorious hair with her nail scissors. She slipped back to bed, and this time, slept.

When she woke the next day she felt much better. She opened some cans and ate. She was horrified to see what she had done to her hair, it stuck out at all angles and looked a mess. She read the papers and magazines that had piled up by the front door. She called her agent. No, he hadn't heard yet. Had she read that Conrad was getting married? She grabbed the papers again, there it was – Conrad Lee – sixty-two years old, famous producer was to marry twenty-year-old model and ex-debutante Shirley Sheldon.

Shirley Sheldon! Claudia gasped in amazement. Shirley Sheldon! Ex-fiancée of the Hon. Jeremy Francis, ex-stripper. It couldn't possibly be true. Shirley was such a drag, a phoney debutante. She always had been interested in getting on in life. She had only hooked up with Jeremy because he was a Hon. Claudia supposed she was going for Conrad's loot, and also because he was fairly famous. But what on earth could he see in her? She wasn't *that* pretty, she had a lousy figure, and she was a dreary bore. The old schmuck must reckon she really was a debutante. What a laugh! Why, she had introduced them. She remembered Shirley coming to her party and having that great suntan, she must have got it in Israel. What a cow! Where had she been the other night? Didn't he involve his fiancée in his orgies? Why not?

Claudia read the article again. The wedding was set for that same day. She just couldn't believe it. Thin Shirley Sheldon, certainly not an ex-debutante, certainly not twenty.

'Ha,' Claudia snorted aloud. It was all too much.

On a sudden impulse she raced to the 'phone booth and looked up the Hon. Jeremy. She found his number and dialled quickly. He was home, stammering and unsure as ever.

'I s-s-say Claudia, how nice,' he said after she announced herself.

'Are you going to Shirley's wedding?' she asked bluntly.

'Oh, I should jolly well s-s-say so, wouldn't want to miss that – w-w-what?!' he chortled happily.

'Well, I thought we might go together,' she said casually, 'It's about time we got together.'

'I say, what a good idea, s-s-shall I fetch you?'

She smiled, it was all too easy. 'Terrific – what time?'

'If the reception s-s-starts at s-s-six, I think if I fetched you at about five-thirty.'

'Marvellous, Jeremy.' She gave him her address and hung up. What an idiot he was.

She spent the afternoon at the hairdresser, and emerged with a whole new look. Her hair, short like a boy's, sleek, with long sideboards. Fortunately it was the look of the moment anyway, all the top models were wearing it. It went well with the ultra short, skimpy gold shift she chose to wear.

Jeremy was impressed. 'I s-s-say, old girl, you look absolutely super!' he said when he called for her.

She fixed him a strong martini and noticed his spotty complexion was still the same. She resisted a strong temptation to ask him if he ever got laid.

'Well, well, so good old Shirley's finally making the wedding bells scene,' she said, sipping at her martini and exhibiting a good deal of leg as she sat in the big armchair opposite Jeremy.

His eyes bulged. 'Yes, I'll s-s-say.'

'Whatever happened with you two?'

'Well,' he waved his long skinny arms about, 'she's a s-s-s-super girl, great fun and all that, but she s-s-said she needed someone more mature.' He took a few gulps of his drink, his Adam's apple bobbing rhythmically, 'We're s-s-still great pals,' he added lamely.

'Just as well,' Claudia said briskly, 'after all, she is much older than you.'

'She is?' Jeremy looked surprised.

'Well, I mean, I don't want to give away any secrets, I mean she looks after herself so well – but after all, how long can she go on fooling everybody?' Claudia shook her head wisely, and Jeremy stared at her, his mouth hanging open inanely. 'Shall we go?' Claudia asked brightly, jumping up and smoothing her dress down.

'Er – yes.' Jeremy got up too. He was very tall and ungainly – a real chinless wonder – Claudia thought, it was no surprise Shirley had ditched him for Conrad, at least Conrad was famous.

Jeremy drove a shiny red M.G. It was very uncomfortable, he had to cram himself behind the wheel.

'Why don't you get a bigger car?' Claudia asked. After all his parents were supposed to be loaded.

'Oh, this little bus really gets around,' he said proudly, 'wouldn't s-s-swop this one in.'

He drove badly, jerking the clutch, cutting up other drivers without even noticing and racing cars at the traffic lights.

Claudia felt sick by the time they arrived. She needed a fast drink. What a joy it would be to see Shirley's and Conrad's faces when they saw her *Quel surprise!*

David sat in his car smoking a cigarette. He didn't have to wait long before a sleek black chauffeur-driven limousine glided to a halt in front of his house – well, Linda's house. A man emerged, David was too far away to recognize him. He swore under his breath and edged his car a little nearer, but it was too late. The man had already gone inside.

Well, Linda was certainly doing all right for herself, the

131

man, whoever he was, obviously had money. Women were such bitches! They couldn't wait – here they were divorced only a few weeks, and there was Linda going out and living it up. Why she'd probably had this sucker all lined up! Cow! She was no better than Claudia. He waited impatiently for them to come out. They were certainly taking their time, probably having a quick one in the living-room. He contemplated going in and punching the man – whoever it was – on the nose. But she probably wouldn't let him in anyway. She would pay for this when he took her back. At the rate she was going maybe he wouldn't even want her back. He sat immersed in his thoughts until they finally came out. The man, the bastard, had his arm around her. The chauffeur jumped out and opened the door for them. They climbed in, the chauffeur got back in the car and they slid off.

David set off in pursuit, keeping a discreet distance between the cars. It was unfortunate for him that at Swiss Cottage the chauffeur decided to skip through a yellow light, and David following him on red, was stopped by a policeman on a motorcycle.

He had to produce his licence and insurance and the policeman gave him a lecture on dangerous driving. Of course, by the time he was free to go their car had long vanished into the night. Pangs of hunger didn't help his mood. He hated eating on his own, but at this hour there seemed no alternative. He decided to go somewhere cheerful so he headed for Carlo's. It was packed as usual. Lots of bright looking birds in their most startling outfits, and the actors, photographers and men about town who were their escorts for the night.

The head waiter told him with a phoney sad shake of his head that it would be at least two hours before he could squeeze in a table for one. David slipped him a pound and the waiter became a little brighter about the prospects. He asked David to wait at the bar, and he would see what he could manage.

David ordered a scotch on the rocks and surveyed the scene. He couldn't help thinking about the last time he had been here with Claudia. He wondered what she was doing now, but he didn't really care; if it hadn't been for her he would be at home with his wife.

A woman was staring at him. He stared back. She had

132

mounds of silver-blonde hair piled on top of her head, and she wore a white mink coat. Her face looked familiar. She was with two men who were in deep conversation – loud old Americans – one had even gone as far as wearing cowboy boots. She sat there, cool, beautiful and remote from her companions.

Suddenly David remembered her. It was Lori Grossman. He put his drink down and went over to her table. 'Hello, Lori,' he said, and then by way of jogging her memory, 'it's David Cooper.'

Her smile was small, sensuous, she extended an elongated whiter than white hand. 'David, how nice.'

The two men stopped talking and she introduced the elder one, he must have been all of seventy, as Marvin Rufus – her husband.

David looked surprised, whatever happened to Jay?

'Sit down – have a drink,' Marvin said, and immediately resumed his conversation with the other man.

Lori slipped off the white mink coat, revealing black lace, cut to a low V. She had small but perfect breasts. She was wearing no bra.

'I ditched Jay,' she said in answer to his unspoken question. 'He was a real cheap bastard.' She adjusted a fabulous diamond bracelet clamped around her thin wrist. 'Marvin knows how to treat a woman . . .' She trailed off, her pale frosty aquamarine eyes staring hungrily into David's.

This one was ready! David congratulated himself on being so attractive to women. She was eating him up with her eyes! 'Linda and I are divorced,' he said, 'just didn't work out.'

'Yeah, I know,' she drawled.

'You know?' he said surprised.

She smiled. 'A little birdie told me and I suppose *you* know that my darling peachy ex is taking out your ex. Isn't that cosy?'

'Jay taking out Linda?' David couldn't believe it.

'That's right, honey.' She moved closer to him and he felt a sudden pressure from her leg under the table. His hand touched a silky thigh. She couldn't wait! Marvin and the other man talked on, something about market prices in London, and would the pound be devalued. 'How long are you here for?' David asked.

'Just a couple of days,' she drawled.

133

That would be long enough. If Jay was knocking off Linda he might as well grab a piece of Lori. She was obviously ready, willing and able.

Under the table his hand crept further up her leg, reaching smooth skin above the stocking top.

'Are you meeting someone?' Lori asked. David shook his head. 'Well, you must join us, Marve won't mind. He'll be talking business for hours.'

In a few minutes their table was ready. True to what Lori had said, her husband continued his marathon conversation with the other man, barely pausing to eat.

Lori ate like a sparrow, nibbling small pieces of steak, picking at a salad. Then the music started and David asked her to dance. She was very tall, her bird's nest of hair making her even more so.

'Well?' he said when they were on the dance floor. The prospect of messing up this spectacular piece of aloofness was exciting him. She felt his excitement and pressed closer.

'Marve will want to go gambling when we leave here, I'll say I'm too tired, and you'll offer to take me to the hotel. We have separate suites there, he won't disturb us.'

He gripped her to him hard, he could feel her bones, she ground her body to the sound of the music sensually.

'What if it doesn't work?' he asked.

'It will work,' she gave a low laugh, 'it always has before.'

Jay 'phoned Linda on Thursday and Friday as he had promised. His 'phone call each day gave her a feeling of well being. He made her feel alive and attractive again.

She rushed around the shops searching for a suitable dress to beguile him with on Saturday night. Everything seemed to have been made for flat-chested seventeen your olds. She finally settled for a very simple white crepe shift, much too expensive, but beautifully cut. She spent the day absorbed in her children, taking them for a long walk on the Heath, and letting them ride on the donkeys. She loved her children, and with Jay in her life she seemed to love them even more.

She took her time getting ready for him – long hot scented bath, careful make-up, freshly combed hair, white crepe dress, few pieces of good jewellery. She couldn't stop herself from thinking about him making love to her. Did he want to? He obviously liked her a lot, would he make a pass at her tonight? Make a pass, what a juvenile thought. She was a divorced woman with two children, not a teenager on a second date. Would he want to sleep with her tonight. That was more like it. She wanted him, she needed him. It had been a long time. Finally she was ready and he was, as usual, on time.

'You look lovely,' he said, 'you don't mind if we stop at a party for a few minutes? Business.'

The party was in Belgravia, an elegant pre-Victorian house, complete with butler and maid at the door. Linda was immediately intimidated. She glanced around the luxurious living-room and recognized several well known faces. The place seemed to be filled with stars and beautiful young girls. Jay knew everyone. He moved around easily, greeting people and Linda trailed miserably behind him, feeling out of place and suddenly plain. To top it all, a gorgeous blonde whom Linda recognized as Susan Standish, put her arm around him intimately and whispered loud enough for Linda to hear – 'You bastard! How dare you leave before I woke up this morning!'

Jay pushed her away, laughing easily.

Linda turned and walked away, nobody seemed interested in talking to her. It was one of those parties where everyone was a 'somebody' in the film industry and unless you were a 'somebody' or a beautiful young starlet, nobody wanted to know. She found a chair and sat down. What a fool she had been. Jay wasn't interested in her, he was probably just sorry for her. She sat brooding. After all, he was a big director, he had the pick of all the girls in London, what could she offer him that he couldn't get more brightly packaged elsewhere? He was heading for her across the room now, she turned on a bright smile, musn't let him see she was upset – embarrass him, what for? There was nothing between them.

'Why did you rush off?' he asked, his eyes faintly amused, 'you left me in the clutches of a female would-be star – always in hot pursuit of us poor old directors. Why didn't you stay and protect me?'

She felt like saying – well you slept with her last night, what do you expect? Instead she just smiled and said, 'I don't know, I thought I'd sit down for a while.'

'We can go in a minute, I just had to put in an appearance otherwise Jan would have never let me forget it.' He pointed to a striking woman in her forties, their hostess.

They left soon after, and dined at a small French restaurant in Chelsea. Before they were half way through their meal, Jay asked her what was wrong. Linda was bad at concealing her feelings, and her manner with Jay had become almost stilted.

'Nothing.' Inexplicably she found her eyes filling with tears.

He changed the subject. 'Let's take the kids out tomorrow, I'm looking forward to meeting them.'

She couldn't think of an excuse. 'All right,' she nodded numbly, 'would you mind awfully if I went home now, I've got a ghastly headache?'

He looked surprised but didn't question her. He paid the bill and they left. Conversation was sparse travelling back to Finchley. Linda found the presence of the chauffeur sitting faceless in the front, a deterrent. At the door she offered Jay her hand and he shook it gravely. 'I'll see you and the kids about twelve tomorrow, we'll take them out to lunch.'

She nodded listlessly. In the morning she would 'phone and put him off.

The wedding reception was crowded.

'Steer me to the bar, I need a drink!' Claudia said at once.

'I s-s-say, shouldn't we try to find them first?' Jeremy stuttered, looking vacantly around.

'No, let's get a drink.'

They headed for the bar. Claudia had a fast glass of champagne, and felt a bit better. She surveyed the crowd, a lot of Shirley's pseudo society friends, rather a tatty-looking group. Here and there were gathered the Americans, the women noticeable in their mink coats or stoles, and the men for their loud voices.

'Dreary looking bunch,' Claudia commented.

Jeremy looked at her vaguely.

A waiter passed with a tray of canapés and Claudia grabbed a few. 'Ugh – lousy food!' she exclaimed, 'a bit of dried up old sausage meat, sort of like the bridegroom!' She giggled, and gulped down some more champagne.

Two tall thin, slightly less spotty replicas of Jeremy approached them. 'J. Francis old chap,' one of them announced loudly, clamping his hand firmly on Jeremy's shoulder and surveying Claudia, 'how are we then?'

'Oh h-h-hello, Robin.'

Robin released his grip on Jeremy. 'Who's your lovely lady then?'

Jeremy waved his arms about, 'Er, Claudia P-p-Parker – this is Robin Humphries.'

'Lord Humphries, old boy, let the girl know who she's talking to.' He smiled at Claudia, revealing a line of crooked nicotine-stained teeth.

She smiled back. She was just starting her fourth glass of champagne.

The other young man pressed anxiously forward. 'I'm Peter Fore-Fitz Gibbons,' he said.

'I say C-c-Claudia,' Jeremy edged between her and Robin and Peter, 'we really should go and look for S-s-Shirley and her h-h-husband.'

'Whatever you say, lover,' Claudia winked at the two young men, 'see you later then. Keep it up.'

They exchanged puzzled looks.

'Funny girl, eh?' Robin said.

'Must be funny to be out with old Jeremy,' Peter agreed.

They watched her as she swayed across the room.

'Wouldn't mind a slice,' Robin said.

'Yes,' agreed Peter.

Claudia had spotted Shirley, and she made her way over to her.

'Shirley! You old dark horse!' She stood firmly in front of her, one hand balancing a glass of champagne, the other holding on to Jeremy.

Shirley didn't bat an eyelid. She smiled politely. 'Claudia darling, such a surprise! So glad you could make it, and Jeremy poppet,' she stood on tiptoe while he placed a sloppy kiss on her cheek, 'divine to see you both.'

'Where's the bridegroom?' Claudia asked, her words slurring slightly.

'Oh, he's around somewhere,' Shirley said brightly. 'Love your hairstyle, darling, wish I could get away with such a harsh cut.'

Claudia smiled. 'Oh, I'm sure you could.'

Jeremy stammered, 'Jolly good show this whole thing.'

Both girls ignored him.

137

'Conrad was telling me about the fun you had the other night,' Shirley said, her voice sugary.

Claudia gave her a sharp look. 'Yes, I thought *you* would be there.'

Shirley giggled softly, 'Why be there when I can see the film.'

'What film?' Claudia's voice became hard.

'Oh, Conrad always takes a film of those evenings.' Shirley smiled triumphantly, 'Didn't you know, it's his hobby actually, you must come over one night and we'll show it to you.'

Claudia stared at her, a horrible sinking feeling in her stomach. She knew Shirley wasn't lying.

'Well, darling,' Shirley continued, 'you did say you wanted to be in his movie.' With a tinkling laugh, she turned away to greet another guest.

Claudia stood there, furious and burning. The son-of-a bitch!

Jeremy said, 'I say, old girl, everything s-s-super?'

She snatched her arm away. 'Oh shut up!'

'What,' Jeremy spluttered, looking hurt.

'Nothing,' she finished the last of her drink and handed Jeremy the empty glass, 'get me some more, will you?'

She had seen Conrad, he was joking and laughing with an elderly couple. She swayed over. 'Hey man,' she said in a loud voice, 'con-grat-ulations.'

His piercing eyes swept over her with disinterest. Shirley walked over and attached herself protectively to his arm.

Claudia smiled at Shirley. 'He's a lousy lay – but then I hear you are too, so that makes it cosy.'

The elderly couple exchanged glances and edged away. Jeremy appeared at that moment with a fresh glass of champagne for her. Claudia took it and held it up to them. 'Here's to a couple of beat-up, fucked-up, old has-beens!'

People nearby were turning to stare.

Conrad said in a low controlled voice, 'Get the hell out of here, you little tramp.'

Claudia smiled. 'My pleasure, you shitless old fart!' She took hold of a startled Jeremy's arm. 'Come on – let's get out of this pissing, boring, wedding!'

A scarlet Jeremy exited with her.

Outside she started to laugh. 'Wasn't that funny? Wasn't that too much?!'

Jeremy stood there, his face still red, his spots standing out angrily. 'I s-s-say, Claudia, how could you. . . .'

'How could I what, man? It was only a giggle.' She suddenly flung her arms around him and kissed him, forcing his stiff lips open with her tongue. 'Come on, let's go back to my place and have some fun.'

Jeremy was reluctant to go, secretly wanting to go back to the wedding reception and apologize, but Claudia insisted. 'I'll show you what it's all about, baby,' she whispered.

Back at her flat she fixed strong drinks, and turned on the record player full blast. Jeremy sat rigid, unsure of himself, while she danced around the room undulating her body and peeling off her dress. She didn't take too much notice of him as she got carried away with the music, she danced and caressed her own breasts, then suddenly ready for him, she came over to where he sat. She began to pull his clothes off. He began to object.

'What are you – a fucking faggot?' she screamed.

He got up and bolted for the door, running off down the stairs like a startled rabbit. Claudia followed him to the top of the stairs yelling after him but he didn't come back. In her drunken haze she was amazed, it was the first time a man – well whatever he was – had turned her down. He had to be queer, those chinless wonder types usually were. She went back into her flat and took a swig out of the scotch bottle. Lousy faggot! How dare he refuse her. Probably couldn't do it. She giggled, and then her eyes inexplicably filled with tears. What was her life about? Where was she getting? It didn't seem to be very far.

All she wanted out of life was to be a star, was that asking so very much? Tears rolled down her cheeks. She turned the music even louder then lay on the floor by the Hi Fi speakers. The volume of the music excited her. She started to manipulate her own body – if that crazy skinny pansy couldn't satisfy her, then she would just have to do it herself. Before she could complete the job she fell into a deep drunken sleep, her snores mingling with the loud sounds of Charlie Parker.

True to what Lori had said after dinner Marvin immediately announced he wanted to gamble. The four of them stood in a huddle on the pavement in front of the restaurant.

'Wanna come and be my lucky charm?' Marvin asked Lori.

She wrapped her mink coat tightly around her and shook her head.

Cowboy boots, anxious to be off, stamped around.

'Well, I guess I'll just play a little craps then,' Marvin said.

'I'll see Lori back to the hotel if you like,' David said quickly, seizing the opportunity.

'That's mighty nice of you,' Marvin boomed. He kissed Lori on the cheek. 'All winnings for you, sugar.' And with a brief handshake to David, he and Cowboy boots were away in a cloud of cigar smoke and resonant Texan drawl. He was obviously a trusting husband, either that or he didn't mind.

Lori laughed. 'Didn't I tell you?'

They walked around the corner to his car, and Lori whispered to him, 'Are you big? I only like big men.'

In the car she acted like a bitch in heat, grabbing for him immediately. He was proud of what he had to offer her. He drove quickly to the hotel. Lori swept through the lobby, haughty and imperial, her white mink drawing envious stares from women. She stopped and greeted an actor she knew. The man gave David an amused look.

Her suite was on the sixth floor, very luxurious, furnished in opulent blue and silver. She threw her mink casually over a chair – 'Make yourself a drink, honey,' she drawled. 'I'm just going to put on something more comfortable.' Her dialogue was straight out of a Hollywood movie! He opened a bottle of champagne that was conveniently on ice and poured two glasses. This was the life! A beautiful woman in beautiful surroundings, champagne, what more could a man ask? She came back soon – wearing a sheer black full length frilled negligée, her hair still piled high. He handed her a glass of champagne and she took a small sip, then lay down on the sofa, the negligée falling back slightly revealing milky white thighs.

He didn't feel quite ready. She held out her arms to him. 'Come to baby, honey,' she drawled. He put his drink down and went over to her.

140

'There's a silk robe in the bathroom,' she purred, 'Why don't you get out of your clothes and be comfortable like me.'

He did feel a bit restricted, and the setting did seem too perfect to start struggling out of his clothes all over the floor. He kissed her on the mouth, tasting her lipstick and then he went to the bathroom and put on the robe she had suggested. It was paisley silk, probably her husband's.

He admired his masculine figure in the mirror, not bad for forty!

She was waiting for him, draped across the sofa looking like a *Vogue* advertisement. He took her in his arms, she put her hands inside his robe scratching his chest gently with talon-like fingernails. He stroked her body, she was very thin with small hard breasts and extended large nipples. An exciting body – not soft and warm like Linda, not curvy and exciting like Claudia. But very sensuous all the same. Like a smooth white snake.

He parted her negligée. Her legs were exceptionally long, crowned at the top by a small mound of silver-blonde hair, matched perfectly to the hair on her head. She opened them slowly, her hands moving round his back, digging her nails into him pulling him closer.

With surprise he realized he wasn't ready. To distract her from this fact he moved his head to her breasts and started to kiss her there. She moaned softly, digging her nails even harder into his back. After a few minutes she grew impatient, and her hands travelled down his body. Her eyes were closed, but they snapped open suddenly when she felt him.

'What's the matter honey?' she purred, a slight edge to her voice, 'this is real Georgia pussy!'

Embarrassed he said. 'It's nothing, just give me a moment.'

Annoyed she closed her eyes again, this time her hands working on him, pulling, stroking, kneading.

'Come on, sugar,' she pleaded, 'this little snatch is waiting for you!'

His physical reaction was nil. This was a nightmare, something that had never happened to him before. He grew panicky, conjuring up every erotic picture he could think of. Nothing, absolutely nothing. He tried to remember the last time he had had sex. Mousey Miss Field, his horrifying

141

secretary. Desperately he thought of the evening he had spent with her.

Suddenly it was all right, he felt himself swelling, growing big, bigger.

Lori sighed with pleasure, 'That's beautiful, honey,' she wrapped her long pale legs around him, and he started to enter her, forcefully, he would show her!

He drove into her, strong brutal thrusts, she squealed with delight, 'Ooh – ooh – that's great, honey – that's wild – ooh – don't stop – don't stop,' her voice changed, 'why have you stopped?'

He didn't reply, he was too overcome with embarrassment. He had heard about this happening to other men, but not to him.

She was getting angry, her sleek sexy drawl was turning shrill.

'What's the matter with you? Are we going to ball or not? If I want this sort of action I can get it with my husband!'

He rolled off her. 'I'm sorry.'

Furious she sat up – 'You're sorry.' She stood up too, her hard breasts and exotic nipples staring accusingly at him. 'Get the hell out of here, I've got to find myself a real man.'

Humiliated, he went to the bathroom and dressed. When he came out she was on the 'phone purring, 'Sure, honey, in ten minutes' time will be fine.'

He let himself out. He was ashamed, what a terrible thing to happen, and why? He had fancied her, strongly fancied her, it wasn't her fault. Although maybe it was, after all she made no secret of the fact that there were many men other than her husband. He went to the bar and ordered a brandy. By the time he had finished it he had convinced himself it was all Lori's fault. Lousy bitch! She had castrated him with thoughts of all the other men. They were all the same, women were all the same. They all wanted to render you impotent in some way or other.

On a sudden impulse he decided to give it another try that night. Not with Lori of course, what about Miss Field Mouse? She was quiet and inoffensive, and he was going to get rid of her anyway, so what harm, one more bash? He didn't even fancy her so it would be real proof if he could make it with her.

142

He vaguely remembered where she lived. She was sure to be home. He had another brandy and set off.

Hammering on her door he found himself as hard as a rock. She got out of bed to answer the door, clutching a woollen dressing-gown around her, lank brown hair, sallow pinched face.

'Mr. Cooper!' she said surprised.

He pushed past her, taking his clothes off and dropping them on the floor. 'Get undressed,' he commanded.

Averting her eyes she obeyed him.

He took her savagely, pinning her puny body to the floor. There was nothing wrong with him!

CHAPTER SEVENTEEN

Linda never did 'phone and cancel Jay the next morning. He came and took them all out to lunch and the children were captivated. He told them stories, played with them and took them to a movie. In the evening he stayed at the house for a bacon and egg supper and Linda found herself unable to break off the relationship. She put Miss Susan Standish to the back of her mind and continued going out with Jay.

She liked him, the children liked him, Janey especially. He was wonderful with them. It became a routine to spend every Sunday together. Jay always thought of new things for them to do, and they looked forward to their day out eagerly. It was a good thing, because since David's last visit he had not been heard from. Linda was furious, it was a pleasure as far as she was concerned, but she thought it selfish and mean of David to completely ignore the children. They were constantly asking, 'When's Daddy coming?' 'Where is he?' If it hadn't been for Jay at week-ends she was sure they would have been a lot more upset. 'Doesn't Daddy love us any more?' Janey asked sadly one afternoon.

'Of course he does, darling,' Linda replied, hugging her little girl to her. 'He's just very busy.'

'I love Uncle Jay,' Janey said solemnly, 'he's not too busy.'

So their relationship flourished, and at the end of a few weeks Linda found herself firmly in love with him. They went to the theatre, small intimate restaurants, large plush restaurants, movies, in fact they spent almost every night together, and regularly every week-end he would spend with her and the children.

Then they went to parties and museums and for drives in the country. He was amusing, attentive, interested in everything she did, but he never attempted more than a brief – almost brotherly – goodnight kiss.

It started to drive her mad. Her body screamed out for some sort of attention. Whenever they danced she would have to hold herself in tight check to prevent herself pushing her body intimately against him. When they kissed she was in suspense waiting for him to go further. But he remained the perfect gentleman. Never touching her.

It reached a point where she decided she could go on no longer. She resolved to bring it up at the next suitable moment. She rehearsed what she would say but it all sounded trite and horrible.

The opportunity came sooner than she expected. There was an end-of-film party at the studio, and Linda was chatting to Jay and Bob Jeffries, the assistant director, when up marched Miss Standish. She was wearing the same white trouser suit Linda had seen her in before. It suited her, complementing her glowing skin and tumbled blonde hair.

'Jay darling,' she murmured, 'can I have a little word with you?'

She had sly eyes, a secret smile always present.

'What is it, Susan?' his tone was pleasant.

'Privately.'

Jay shrugged his shoulders at Linda and Bob and walked away with Susan.

Linda said, 'Is she in the film?'

Bob laughed. 'At the moment she is but I've got a feeling she's going to land on the cutting-room floor.'

'Oh,' Linda quickly changed the subject, she didn't want Bob to think she was jealous.

Jay returned quite soon and didn't mention the incident,

but Linda knew that as soon as they were alone she was going to bring it up.

After the party, joined by Bob Jeffries and his wife they went to Annabels. It was impossible to talk there, and on the drive home there was the ever present chauffeur.

'You're very withdrawn tonight,' Jay said, his tone light. She nodded.

'What's the matter?' he was concerned.

'I don't want to talk now,' she said looking towards the chauffeur. 'Come in for coffee if you like.'

She had never invited him into her house when he took her home before, and she felt a little strange about it. She sat him down in the living-room and went into the kitchen. Now that she had him there what was there to say? It was all so difficult, there were no words that could really express the way she felt.

Absently she placed some chocolate biscuits on a plate, and filled the coffee jug. He was sitting reading the evening paper. She felt at a complete loss for words as she handed him his coffee. He solved the problem for her by speaking first.

'I have to go back to Los Angeles in two weeks.'

'Oh,' she felt deflated.

He hesitated and then said, 'How about coming with me?'

'With you?' For a few pleasant seconds she considered the possibility, then reality hit her. 'That's impossible, Jay, I couldn't leave the children.'

'Well, bring the children then, they'd love it there.'

She shook her head. 'I couldn't take them out of school anyway....'

He cut her short, 'Linda, I'm not very good at this sort of thing, I've only ever said it to idiots before,' he got up nervously, 'Linda, I'm asking you to marry me.' He rushed on, 'I love you very much, you're the most wonderful warm giving woman I've ever met. I know you've been burnt once and I know how you feel about men – but believe me I'll try to make you happy. I'm not perfect. I've been involved with a lot of stupid broads – I've got a weakness for tall blondes I can't deny – but if you'll marry me I think everything will work out and I think we could make a wonderful life together.' He paused, 'Well?'

'Jay,' she whispered his name. 'Yes, Jay, yes, yes.'

145

He kissed her. 'Let's do it soon, baby, like tomorrow. I can't wait for you much longer.'

She felt tears stinging her eyes. 'I love you.'

He stroked her hair then let her go. 'Go to bed, I'll call you first thing. I'll arrange everything, the sooner the better, huh?'

She nodded. 'The sooner the better,' she murmured.

*   *   *

Claudia spent the next few days after Shirley and Conrad's wedding in a drunken stupor. She drank a full bottle of scotch a day, occasionally cramming her mouth with sleeping pills or tranquillizers until she reached a sort of happy oblivion. She didn't eat, wash or dress but wandered around the apartment in a sordid naked splendour.

The 'phone rang but she never picked it up. One day the door buzzer rang so insistently that she was forced to answer it.

It was Giles – 'Christ!' He was aghast at her appearance. He bundled her into a dressing-gown and made her drink black coffee until her eyes started to focus and she could talk.

'What kind of a trip have you been on?' he asked.

She shook her head. 'Man, I feel terrible.'

'You look terrible.'

'What day is it?'

'Oh, God, you've really been away, it's Monday.'

'Monday, I guess I went on a little bender.'

He surveyed the room, empty scotch bottles, broken records, overturned furniture. 'I guess so, who was the guy?'

She shrugged. 'No one. Just felt like getting stoned alone. What are you doing here anyway? Thought you were in Spain.'

'I've come bearing glad tidings. Your tits are world famous.' He produced a copy of *Man at Play*, one of the biggest selling men's magazines in the States. He opened it and showed her the centre fold-out. There she was in solid colour standing on her terrace with London silhouetted in the background, wearing the pink shirt which Giles had hosed with water. Her perfect rounded breasts standing out firm and full, the nipples rigid and pointed. He turned the page, there she was lying on her bed, black negligée filming around her, her breasts escaping, mouth half open, eyes half closed. The next page and the next page were all of her. The caption said 'Beautiful London model and actress Claudia Parker shows us some of the better sights of Great Britain!'

'You're a big hit,' Giles said enthusiastically, 'they want us to do a whole new series of photos. They'll pay a bomb. Want us to fly to New York. Want you to meet Edgar J. Pool – owner of the magazine. This is your big chance, baby, this is successville.'

She studied the magazine, why, oh why, had she cut her hair? 'When do we go?' she asked, her face lighting up.

'As soon as we get you into shape. You look scrawny as hell and that hair, we'll have to get you a wig. Here, sign this.' He thrust a paper at her which she signed without so much as a glance. 'I'm going to book you into this health farm for a week, you really need it. I reckon about ten days from now we can go. I'll let them know. They're really wild for you – want you to be Miss Playgirl of the Year. Baby, you and I are going to be rich.

Was it the fifth or sixth night David had spent with Miss Field? He couldn't remember. He only knew it had become a habit to leave the office, eat dinner, have a few drinks and then go hammering on her door.

She held a sort of morbid fascination for him. What was it about her that made sex so overpowering and exciting. It was certainly the most erotic sensation he had ever had. She always crept to the door clutching her woollen dressing-gown to her, he always had to command her to undress, and she took her clothes off reluctantly, revealing a thin white undernourished body. She was flat chested with flaccid nipples that didn't even harden to the touch.

However, when he was in her, pounding away, she held him in a grip of steel, squeezing and pumping the life out of him. Giving him no rest, holding him in her like a vice.

He tried to humiliate her by forcing her into ludicrous positions, but she took to them all with no argument. He hated her but he couldn't stop returning there night after night.

During the day at the office neither of them mentioned it. She crept around quietly going about her business mouse-like as usual.

He wanted to break the habit.

A busy provocative-looking girl called Ginny was doing

an ad. for his company. He manoeuvred an introduction to her. He found her very attractive, she reminded him of a much sexier more obvious version of Claudia.

He invited her out to dinner. She turned up in an almost topless startlingly red dress. She had very pink and white skin, and full pouty lips. This was going to be all right, he decided.

During dinner she drank frozen daquiris and giggled a lot. They danced, and her body was warm and bouncy. All the men in the restaurant were watching her, which made David feel good. At one point, during a vigorous shake, one full pink and white breast popped completely over the top of her dress, giving a full view of a pale brown nipple, wide and generous. She tucked herself back into her dress with an inane giggle.

David felt the time had come to take her back to his hotel. She put up little objection, and once there it was an easy job to peel her out of her red dress. She was wearing frilly pink panties underneath, and her body was like an overgrown cupid. Her breasts were so big and bouncy and unbelievable that he had a sneaky suspicion that they weren't breasts at all, just a lot of silicone injections put together.

He couldn't do anything, there was no excitement. Still giggling she was given money for a taxi and sent home.

He went to bed, couldn't sleep, until at last he was forced to get up and visit his Miss Field. By the time he got there his excitement was at such a peak that he hardly made it on top of her.

She had a strange power over him.

He tried with several other women, but each time the same result. His life began to revolve around Harriet Field.

He found out about her. She was thirty years old and had been with the firm for twelve years working her way up from the typing pool to become his private secretary. There was no gossip about her, she kept herself to herself, she was the office nonentity.

When he went to her at night they never talked, he just told her what to do and she did it, whatever it was. Sometimes, after, politely she would ask him if he would care for coffee or tea, he would always say no, and as soon as he could summon the strength he would get up and go.

He wondered what she thought about it all. Why did she

148

never say anything? The whole thing was very unnatural. Then next time, of course, was later that same evening. He went earlier than usual, and she was still up, clutching a skimpy cardigan around her non-existent bosom. Automatically she started to undress. It was the first time he had ever seen her get out of her clothes, usually it was just a night-gown and dressing-gown. There seemed to be layers of them, cardigan, jumper, a vest (one of the most unattractive garments he had ever seen), salmon pink bra, skirt slip, long woollen drawers, smaller pants, suspender belt and thick stockings. Shivering slightly she stood before him.

She was certainly a randy bitch, he thought, always prepared, always creamed up and ready to go. Probably been frustrated for years. Maybe he should make her wait for it tonight. She was already lying on the floor, opening pale sluggish legs. He couldn't make her wait, the burning desire he felt wouldn't let him, he ripped off his clothes hurriedly and crouched on top of her. She heaved a big sigh and they were away.

Afterwards she put on her dressing-gown and started to tidy his clothes, piling them neatly together, ready for him to put on.

He lay watching her, she really was plain, it wasn't that she made the worst of herself, it was just that there was nothing one could do to improve her. She noticed him looking at her and flushed.

'Tea or coffee, Mr. Cooper?'

'Both,' he said abruptly. She turned to go into the kitchen and he had a feeling she would bring him both if he didn't stop her. 'Sit down,' he said. She sat hesitantly, crossing her feet at the ankles, clasping her hands on her lap in front of her. 'I want to talk to you.'

They sat silently. After he had said he wanted to talk to her, he suddenly realized he didn't want to talk to her at all, he just wanted to go.

'It doesn't matter,' he said abruptly.

'Is something wrong, Mr. Cooper?'

'For God's sake don't call me Mr. Cooper.'

She lowered her eyes. 'Yes, David dear.'

Christ, she acted like a vestal virgin, she became so coy and retiring. He stood up, decisions filtering through his mind. He would fire her on Monday and this was positively the last time.

Maybe he should hammer it into her once more since this was the last visit. 'Get across the table,' he said wearily.

Linda and Jay were married a week later at Hampstead register office. Quietly with no fuss. Linda's parents were there, surprised but happy. The children dressed in their best clothes were strangely subdued. A few friends of Jay's and a few of Linda's.

Afterwards they all went back to Jay's hotel suite and ate wedding cake and drank champagne and chatted. It was very small, very informal. Soon Linda's parents said they should be starting the drive back to the country. They gathered together the children, who were going to stay with them, and all said goodbye.

Linda hugged Janey and Stephen to her. 'Mummy won't be away very long and then we're all going to live together in a beautiful big house with a swimming pool in America.'

'Wow – a swimming pool!' Stephen said delightedly.

Janey was fighting back tears, her little innocent chubby face concerned and worried. 'I hope the plane doesn't crash, Mummy.'

Linda laughed and hugged her. 'Don't be a silly baby.'

Jay picked up Janey and kissed her. 'You be a good little girl and Mummy will be back before you know it.'

Janey looked at him with big brown eyes. 'Are you my new daddy?'

Jay nodded solemnly. Janey kissed him and scampered off to her grandparents. Soon the rest of the guests departed and they were alone.

Linda took off her hat and sighed, 'I hate leaving the children.'

Jay laughed. 'It's only for a couple of weeks, you don't mind if I have a little time alone with my wife.'

'No I don't mind,' she smiled at him, 'I love you, Jay.'

There were several telegrams, one from Conrad and Shirley Lee honeymooning in Mexico – 'Congratulations, English wives are the best they don't want so much alimony. Love regards Conrad and Shirley.' A sarcastic one from his fifteen-year-old daughter Caroline, 'Best wishes Daddy on your fourth wife, Caroline.'

'She's a fresh kid,' Jay said grimly.

'Why do you say that?' Linda enquired.

'I don't know,' he shrugged. 'I guess it's my fault really.

She's a tough little cookie – takes after her mother. I never spent any time with her, and Jenny never re-married, so I suppose it's affected her not having a father around.'

'I'd like to meet her,' Linda said quietly, 'maybe when we're settled she could come and stay with us for a while.'

'Forget it,' Jay laughed brusquely, 'her mother would never allow it, anyway, she's not a child any more, it's too late for me to start stepping in the picture.'

'She's only fifteen, Jay, I think we should try it.'

He kissed her. 'You're sweet.'

She smiled and changed the subject. 'I hope I've brought the right clothes for Jamaica, it's all been such a rush.'

'Are you sorry?'

'Sorry? What a ridiculous thing to say, of course I'm not.'

'Let's have dinner up here, the car will be picking us up at six a.m., we'd better get an early night.'

'That's a wonderful idea,' she yawned, 'I think I'll take a bath now.'

'Leave it to me, I'll order you something special.'

She went into the bedroom. Her two suitcases and make-up case were stacked neatly at the bottom of one of the twin beds. Twin beds, how awful, she wondered how they'd manage.

She hoped she wasn't going to be a big disappoinment to Jay. He was used to such beautiful women. She remembered elegant cool Lori. Perhaps it would have been better to have slept together before getting married. Then at least he would have known what he was getting. But he hadn't wanted that, although they hadn't actually discussed it she knew he didn't want that.

She unpacked a long blue silk nightdress and matching robe. It flattered her, plunging between her heavy breasts and swirling down to the floor clingingly. She took a long bath, carefully removing her daytime make-up and putting on a lighter one. She brushed her thick auburn hair, it was growing and reached almost to her shoulders. Her body and face were by no means perfect, but she was an attractive sensual-looking woman.

Jay had ordered more champagne, a delicious fish course, and thin slivers of perfectly white chicken in a cream wine and mushroom sauce on a bed of rice. Afterwards there were strawberries Romanoff and large goblets of Courvoi-

151

sier brandy. After dinner Linda was bathed in a gloriously happy glow. Jay seemed to make everything perfect.

He took her to the bedroom and undressed her slowly, he made love to her beautifully. Nothing frantic, nothing rushed. He caressed her body as though there was nothing more important in the world. He took her to the edge of ecstacy and back again, keeping her hovering, sure of every move he made. Her breasts grew under his touch, swelling, becoming even larger and firmer. She floated on a suspended plane, a complete captive to his hands and body. He had amazing control, stopping at just the right moment. When it did happen it was only because he wanted it to, and they came in complete unison. She had never experienced *that* before, and she clung to him, words tumbling out of her mouth about how much she loved him. Afterwards they lay and smoked and talked. 'You're wonderful,' he said, 'you're a clever woman making me wait until after we were married!'

'What?' She snuggled closer to him.

'Well, I wanted you very much, but I knew if I made a wrong move I'd become just another guy on the make. You know I laid Lori the first time I saw her. She came for an interview, we locked the office door and made it then and there. Can you imagine marrying a broad you screwed as soon as you met. That's what kind of schmuck I was until I met you, and realized what a real woman was like.'

She kissed him. 'But weren't you worried if we'd – well – like each other in bed, I mean why didn't you try before?'

'Because I wasn't about to take no for an answer!'

'But I might not have said no!'

He agreed. 'No, you might not have, but you're not the sort of woman to have an affaire, you would have regretted it and I would have become the bad one in your mind.'

'Oh,' she was amazed at how well he knew her. He was probably right.

'What about Susan Standish?' she asked accusingly.

'I'm a man, Linda,' he said simply, 'don't expect me to make excuses, she was a nice girl and I couldn't have you.'

Her eyes were closing. 'I love you, husband,' she murmured, and soon she was asleep.

The health farm wasn't too bad. It was a nice place to relax, to think, to take stock. Claudia submitted her body to

152

the care of the experts, and within a few days her physical appearance was back to normal. She spent her days between massage and therapy, sunning herself beside the luxurious swimming pool in the grounds. The early English sun was weak but restful. She daydreamed a lot of the time, imagining herself a star, a success. That was all she really wanted out of life, was it too much to ask?

Giles came to visit her. 'You look great!' he said enthusiastically. 'Just like the girl I used to know.'

He had a lot of correspondence from the magazine, eagerly waiting her arrival.

'You've really made a big impression on *someone* there,' he said cheerfully, 'they can't wait. Planning promotions for you all over the place. They want to feature you as Miss Playgirl of the Year.'

Claudia was delighted. Maybe this was the opportunity she had been waiting for.

Soon she was ready to leave the farm. Giles took her back to his studio flat in Chelsea. 'I've moved all your things out of the penthouse,' he told her, 'it's not a good scene for you, you'll stay with me 'til we go.'

She was pleased. Giles was taking over, and she liked it.

They slept in a big sprawling bed like brother and sister, and during the day Giles took her shopping for new clothes, and she bought a fabulous shiny ash-blonde wig to cover her own cropped hair until it grew back.

He paid for everything. 'An investment,' he told her airily.

Eventually he decided they were ready to go, and he wired the magazine. He received a lengthy cabled reply, they had already sent the tickets. The reply said, 'Be Prepared Big Welcome For Future Miss Playgirl. All Press alerted. Party planned for p.m. of your arrival.'

Claudia was delighted. New York awaited her.

It was just no good, David couldn't break the habit of Harriet Field.

He found it absolutely impossible to get an erection with any other woman. He tried religiously, even going so far as to take a girl to a pornographic show in the hope that that would excite him enough. The only result of that was that the girl got so worked up that when he couldn't satisfy her she called him every name under the sun.

He felt if he could only make it with anyone other than Harriet Field, the spell would be broken. But no, it remained an impossible feat, and sex with Harriet got better and better.

He took to staying at her apartment all night, and now he found he had to have her in the morning too. He became white and insipid-looking, and slowly she seemed to be draining the strength from him.

He would wake up in the cramped apartment, bad tempered and uncomfortable. It was obvious that if he was going to continue this relationship he would have to make other arrangements about her living quarters. He didn't want to set her up in a flat, but it seemed the only answer.

She never said anything to him when they weren't having sex, she kept well out of his way. She sort of hovered, which infuriated him.

He usually drove her to the office dropping her about a block away, and she would huddle on her seat in the car, mouse-like and silent.

He hated her, but he couldn't leave her. Was it never going to end, this mad animal desire he had for this wretched creature?

He hadn't seen his children, somehow he felt ashamed to face them.

His life was one long round of work, to which he threw himself into wholeheartedly, and sex with Harriet. Otherwise he slept.

He got very thin and haggard-looking. It's got to end soon, he reasoned with himself, I'll just keep going until I've had so much of her it will be over.

He ignored everything else and concentrated on getting Harriet out of his system. This involved sleeping with her at every possible opportunity, and now, even at the office he would sometimes lock the door and take her quickly on the floor or across his desk. It didn't help. It just seemed to make her more exciting.

He plodded on, determined to finish the affaire.

At London airport Claudia was besieged by photographers.

'Look this way', 'Look over here', 'Pull your skirt up a bit,' 'Let's see some leg.'

154

Claudia obliged, she was wearing a very short skirt with matching coat, and clingy silk sweater.

Giles stood watching. He knew he made a smart move getting her to sign the personal management contract. Now he had fifty per cent of her, and he had a hunch that fifty per cent was going to mean an awful lot of loot.

The Americans were about to discover a new sex symbol. She would bowl them over. Whereas in England she was just looked on as another little starlet, she had the potential to be a big star. Giles was sure of this. With the right exposure and the right publicity he had it made. He would have to watch her closely, see she didn't drink too much, didn't get laid by the wrong people. She was smiling sexily at the photographers, her head thrown back, lips parted, slanty green eyes shining. She blossomed even more in the spotlight. Her bosom strained to escape from the thin confines of her sweater, her legs were long and shapely.

'Come on baby, we'll miss the plane,' Giles said at last.

She gave the photographers one last provocative pose, then took Giles' hand, squeezing it firmly – 'This is a ball!' she exclaimed.

In another part of the airport Linda and Jay sat in a V.I.P. lounge sipping coffee. Jay's was laced with a good stiff shot of whisky. He hated flying and found the only way he could climb on a plane was to be mildly stoned. Linda admired her wedding ring, a thin band of perfect diamonds. She could hardly believe how much she loved this man. After David the thought of being able to pick up the pieces and start again had seemed impossible. Now, the ten years with David seemed almost non-existent.

Jay took her hand. 'You look beautiful today.'

She smiled. 'Thank you.'

A stewardess arrived and told them it was time to board the plane. A lone photographer stopped them in the hall, 'Is it possible to have a picture, Mr. Grossman?'

'Sure,' Jay smiled amicably, and put his arm around Linda.

She was surprised. 'Why do they want your picture?' she whispered.

'The studio usually arranges it. Another plug for the movie.'

'Oh,' she nodded wisely.

They sat in comfort on the plane, Jay taking furtive swigs out of a silver hip flask. Then the great engines began to roar, and the plane taxied gently off down the runway.

One morning David woke up in a particularly foul temper. His head ached, and the room smelt of stale sex – Harriet never seemed to open any windows. He reached for her immediately, his physical feelings overcame anything else.

After satisfying himself he felt even worse.

She made him coffee and gave him the morning paper. He smoked a cigarette and glanced at the paper. On the front page was Claudia. She faced the camera three-quarters on, bosom thrust out, hair long and wild, amused knowing smile. She looked gorgeous, shapely legs disappearing into a short skirt. 'Beautiful model and actress Claudia Parker (21) leaves for New York today. Miss Parker plans to discuss film offers. She is travelling with Giles Taylor, well known avant garde fashion and society photographer. Both deny a romance.' David felt anger – anger that she should look so good and appear so happy. After he had left her he had imagined she would go to pieces, vanish from his life.

But there she was on the front page, off to America, without apparently, a care in the world.

Little bitch! She had ruined his marriage. He turned the page in a fury, why couldn't she just have faded into oblivion?

There on the next page was a small picture of Linda with a man. She looked çalm and smiling, and the man held her arm protectively.

'Mr. Jay Grossman, well known Hollywood director, and the new Mrs. Grossman leave for a honeymoon in Jamaica. Mr. Grossman has just finished making "Besheba" here and on location in Israel.'

Mrs. Jay Grossman – it was impossible. How dare she! He studied the picture intently, searching her face for signs of unhappiness, but there were none – she was serene and confident and very attractive. How could she do it without telling him? Then he remembered last week she had left three messages at the office for him to 'phone her, and he hadn't bothered to return her calls. He hadn't even seen the children for weeks.

'Blast.' He swore angrily. He had always imagined that Linda would be available when he did decide to settle down. She would take him back. Harriet Field had delayed his thoughts about getting back with Linda. He had drifted into this sordid affaire with her, and everything else had been neglected. He hadn't even thought about seeing his children.

He felt trapped, what could he do? There was no Linda to save him now. The time had come to run. He thought of the words of a children's song – Run Rabbit – run rabbit – run run run – and they repeated in his mind with an insistent monotony.

There were retching sounds coming from the bathroom, soon Harriet came into the room. Unusual for her, she hadn't dressed yet, but was clutching her faded woollen robe around her.

She stood in front of him, white and wretched-looking. 'We are with child,' she stated blankly.

He stared at her in panic and slowly he realized it was too late to run, the trap was closing.

0352   Star

396423	Mary Ann Ashe **RING OF ROSES**	60p
396938	Andre P. Brink **LOOKING ON DARKNESS**	95p
39613X	William Burroughs **DEAD FINGERS TALK**	75p
398663	Jackie Collins **THE WORLD IS FULL OF DIVORCED WOMEN**	50p
398752	**THE WORLD IS FULL OF MARRIED MEN**	50p
300671	Eric Corder **HELLBOTTOM**	75p*
300086	**THE LONG TATTOO**	40p*
398515	**RUNNING DOGS**	60p*
396113	Robertson Davies **FIFTH BUSINESS**	95p
396857	Terry Fisher **IF YOU'VE GOT THE MONEY**	70p
39840X	Knight Isaacson **THE STORE**	60p
396105	Gavin Lambert **IN THE NIGHT ALL CATS ARE GREY**	75p
396334	**THE SLIDE AREA**	75p
398299	Robin Maugham **THE SIGN**	55p*
397594	Clayton Moore **END OF RECKONING**	60p*
397608	**141 TERRACE DRIVE**	60p*
397543	**RIVER FALLS**	60p*
397667	**SECRET FIRE**	60p*
397659	**THE CORRUPTERS**	60p*
397551	**WESLEY SHERIDAN**	60p*
300809	Molly Parkin **LOVE ALL**	50p
397179	**UP TIGHT**	60p
396946	Judith Rossner **TO THE PRECIPICE**	85p*

†For sale in Britain and Ireland only.
*Not for sale in Canada.

GENERAL FICTION

397144	Alan Sillitoe THE FLAME OF LIFE	70p
398892	THE GENERAL	50p
300965	THE LONELINESS OF THE LONG DISTANCE RUNNER	50p
300949	MEN, WOMEN AND CHILDREN	50p
398809	THE RAGMAN'S DAUGHTER	50p
300981	SATURDAY NIGHT AND SUNDAY MORNING	50p
396415	Hubert Selby Jr. THE ROOM	75p
398884	Ernest Tidyman STARSTRUCK	60p*

0426   Tandem

162560	Gerty Agoston MY BED IS NOT FOR SLEEPING	50p*
175824	Nigel Balchin THE BORGIA TESTAMENT	60p
175905	THE SMALL BACK ROOM	60p
176030	MINE OWN EXECUTIONER	60p
176111	A SORT OF TRAITORS	60p
180593	Bill Bavin THE DESTRUCTIVE VICE	75p
163796	Catherine Cookson THE GARMENT	60p
163524	HANNAH MASSEY	60p
163605	SLINKY JANE	60p
162803	Jean Francis COMING AGAIN	45p*
182278	John Goulet THE HUMAN APE	75p*
165209	Brian Hayles SPRING AT BROOKFIELD	50p
172167	Harrison James ABDUCTION	50p*
151577	Julie Lawrence BLONDES DON'T HAVE ALL THE FUN!	50p*
16539X	Keith Miles AMBRIDGE SUMMER	50p
178815	Betty Smith JOY IN THE MORNING	70p*
179455	MAGGIE: NOW	75p*
178734	TOMORROW WILL BE BETTER	70p*

†For sale in Britain and Ireland only   *Not for sale in Canada.

	Gordon Boshell		
113918	**THE BLACK MERCEDES**		60p
114043	**THE MILLION POUND RANSOM**		60p
117468	**THE MENDIP MONEY-MAKERS**		60p
	Graeme Cook		
105087	**COMMANDOS IN ACTION!**	(illus) (NF)	35p
	Terrance Dicks		
	THE MOUNTIES:		
110927	**THE GREAT MARCH WEST**		40p
	THE MOUNTIES:		
111052	**MASSACRE IN THE HILLS**		40p
	THE MOUNTIES:		
111133	**WAR DRUMS OF THE BLACKFOOT**		45p
	G. Krishnamurti		
103645	**THE ADVENTURES OF RAMA**		35p
	John Lucarotti		
11535X	**OPERATION PATCH**		45p

Animal Stories

	Judith M. Berrisford		
107004	**SKIPPER AND SON**	(illus)	35p
107276	**SKIPPER'S EXCITING SUMMER**		40p
	Molly Burkett		
118502	**FOXES, OWLS AND ALL** (illus)		70p
111567	**THAT MAD, BAD BADGER ...**	(NF)	35p
	Constance Taber Colby		
109899	**A SKUNK IN THE FAMILY**	(illus) (NF)	45p
	G. D. Griffiths		
113675	**ABANDONED!**	(illus)	35p
	David Gross		
117549	**THE BADGERS OF BADGER HILL**		50p
	Sara Herbert		
109627	**THE PONY PLOT**		35p
109708	**THE SECRET OF THE MISSING FOAL**		35p
	Alex Lea		
107861	**TEMBA DAWN, MY CALF**		30p
	Joyce Stranger		
11017X	**THE SECRET HERDS**	(illus)	45p
	Alison Thomas		
115511	**BENJI**		40p

†For sale in Britain and Ireland only.
*Not for sale in Canada.